MOONLIGHT AND MOUNTAINS

STONECROFT SAGA 4

B.N. RUNDELL

Moonlight And Mountains

Paperback Edition

Wolfpack Publishing
6032 Wheat Penny Avenue
Las Vegas, NV 89122

wolfpackpublishing.com

This book is a work of fiction. Any references to historical events, real people or real places are used fictitiously. Other names, characters, places and events are products of the author's imagination, and any resemblance to actual events, places or persons, living or dead, is entirely coincidental.

Paperback ISBN 978-1-64734-497-9
eBook ISBN 978-1-64734-171-8

MOONLIGHT AND MOUNTAINS

DEDICATION

Time. We have so little of it. The Bible says we can only expect threescore and ten years, or seventy years, and if by good fortune we enjoy fourscore, then we are blessed indeed. But in those years, every day is made up of tiny moments of time. Tiny moments that we all too often squander. When I think of that time, I cannot help but think of the time that is spent staring at the dim glow of a computer screen and letting my fingers linger over the keys as my mind dances through the tangled webs of cluttered thought, trying to sort out the real from the imaginary. But I also know that every moment I spend with the fictional figures in the books, I have robbed those moments from other endeavors. And for that reason, I once again dedicate this book to my beloved wife, who has so unselfishly shared my time, my tiny moments, with those who might someday read these very words with little thought to the precious moments of my life and the life of my dear partner that have been surrendered to this work. Thank you, my beloved. You and every moment with you will be forever treasured.

1 / Arapaho

It was a downcast lot that rode strung out in the bottom of the dry gulch. They rode into the rising sun. Black Eagle was in the lead, the proven war leader of the Arapaho village led by her father, Chief Sitting Elk. The land was dry, game was scarce, and the people were hungry. It had been an open winter with less snowfall than had been seen in many years and even the buffalo had not come north, staying in the southern lands where the grass was green and plentiful.

"This is the moon when the buffalo bellow, but there are none. What will we do?" asked Three Toes. He was one of two sons of the brother of her mother, White Calf, and the two brothers always accompanied her on any hunts or raids. But this was the third hunt in this moon and the band of ten hunters had only three deer to show for their effort. It was not enough meat for the village of thirty lodges; perhaps the other hunting party would be more successful.

Black Eagle looked at her cousin, "We will go again. If the

buffalo do not come, we must go south to the buffalo!" She spoke with confidence, but inside she felt only fear, fear for her people that depended on her and the other warriors to provide for and protect the people. The village of the Arapaho lay beneath the tall peak in the range of mountains that would one day be called Laramie Mountains, but now was known only as the summer camp of the band of Sitting Elk.

It was proving to be a season of testing for the people. Shortly after their move to the higher ground when the snow retreated, they had been raided by a large band of Utes. Two of their own were killed and they lost twenty-two horses. But the Utes were after women and their raid had been repulsed and they settled for the stolen horses. It had often been said the shorter, stout built Utes were an ugly people and would try to steal women from the Arapaho to make their people more attractive, for the Arapaho were a handsome race with tall strong men and beautiful women.

And now, with the buffalo herds not coming north, they were facing a season of starving. Even the deer and other animals had moved to greener lands and now the village would also have to move, just to survive. But that was a decision to be made by her father and the council of seven, sometimes referred to as the seven old men, even though there were women among them.

Three Toes suddenly reined up, pointing to the ground in front of them, "Ho! Those are tracks of those we saw before!" The tracks of four horses crossed the bottom of the gulch and climbed the clay soil bank and over the shoulder of the mountain. “These are two, three days old,” declared Three Toes, he was on a knee beside the tracks, having felt the soil and tested the sides of the tracks. “These are deep, the horses are carrying heavy,” he paused, looked at the tracks that disappeared over the ridge, “Should we go after them? They might have much we could use.”

“No,” stated Black Eagle. “We are near our village and we must take the meat to them. If my father says, we will return and go after these intruders.”

“We could send the others to the village and we could go after these!” he suggested, excitedly, hoping for a chance to earn honors by taking an enemy of the people.

“We do not know these are enemies and we do not know what they carry. We will go to the village first!” declared Black Eagle in a tone that allowed no argument. Three Toes swung back aboard his mount, looked back at the tracks and gigged his horse forward. He fell back from Black Eagle, unhappy with her response, but knowing he could not dispute her decision. He, of course, could chose to go alone but by rebelling against her leadership, he would not be chosen for any other raids or hunts in the future and she was the most successful war leader among their people.

Black Eagle reined up and called Three Toes forward. “You and your brother, Many Feathers, follow those,” she pointed toward the tracks discovered by Three Toes. “Do not attack! Return with the word of who they are and what they are doing here, if you can.” Three Toes grinned, motioned to his brother, and the two warriors took off at a canter, following the tracks over the shoulder of the mountain.

***

"This ain't the smartest thing we've ever done!" exclaimed Ezra, watching his friend trying to negotiate the slide rock. They had been traveling by moonlight for the past week, preferring to limit their chances of being spotted by any natives that might not appreciate their presence. But moonlight and slide rock are not compatible, especially with horses and riders, neither of which are familiar with the hazard common to the mountains.

Gabe had been astride his big black Andalusian stallion when he moved out of the aspen grove to cross the face of the mountain where the teetering and unstable slide rock gave them a quick education on the hazards of impulsive decisions. And when Ebony, the big black, slipped and dropped to his knees, launching Gabe over his head to land painfully on the jagged moss-covered slabs, they failed the first test of mountain riding.

Gabe struggled to his feet, felt his arms and legs, wincing from the pain and realizing he was going to have a number of bruises, and walked back to Ebony just as the horse rose to his feet, trembling and looking at the granite slabs. Big eyes stared at Gabe as he stroked the head and neck of his beloved horse, speaking softly to calm the big animal, as he looked around for a safer way to get back to the trees.

He chose to return the twenty plus feet to the trees following the same route, but now he had to get Ebony turned around. With a strong hand on the reins, he moved slightly uphill, just enough for the horse to turn around, but even here the rocks were unstable. Gabe tested each one, bent down to pick one up and tossed it aside, then continued. Ebony bent around, took some tentative steps and once straight, and with Gabe leading, they moved back to the security of the aspen grove.

Gabe breathed a deep sigh of relief, rolling his shoulders with the pain, and wincing with every step because of the hard crack he took on his kneecap with his less than graceful landing. He looked at his friend, "Let's make camp in those trees, and we'll wait till daylight before we go any further."

"Now that's the smartest thing you've said all night!" replied Ezra, grinning at the aches and pains of his friend.

Oftentimes it is difficult to find a clearing in a grove of aspen. The quakies, as they are also called because of the movement of the leaves in the wind, grow close together, so close that it is difficult for anything to move between them, but that is usually in a new growth with many saplings. The long-standing growths with mature trees are excellent places of shelter and cover. The two friends found a small clearing, close to the chuckling stream that cascaded from the mountain top and made their camp. Gabe tended the four horses as Ezra made the cookfire and started the coffee.

The two men had been traveling together for over a year with their ultimate goal that of exploring the uncharted wilderness of the west and to see the Rocky Mountains.

Lifelong friends, the men were nothing alike. Gabe, or Gabriel Stonecroft, was raised in a prominent family with all the benefits of wealth including a university education. A tall broad-shouldered blonde headed man, he had also been schooled in boxing by the champions Daniel Mendoza and Gentleman John Jackson, and while in England, he also had instruction in the Yōshin-ryū style of Jujitsu. With a natural skill with weapons, and a confidence born of experience, Gabe was a man that could handle himself in just about any scrape and had done so often enough.

It was an offense against his sister that caused this well-known figure in Philadelphia society to defend the honor of his sister and his family name against a blowhard bully that thought he, because of his position and family connections, could do whatever he wanted to whomever he pleased. The two men met in a duel that resulted in the death of Jason Wilson, the son of a member of the Second Continental Congress and the nephew of Supreme Court Justice John Rutledge. Although Gabriel did all he could to avoid the fight and had adhered to the *Code Duello,* his opponent did not and was killed.

When Wilson's vengeance seeking father put a bounty on Gabriel's head, the better part of valor demanded he leave Philadelphia for the protection of his family, his sister, Gweneth, now married and moved to Washington, and his father, Boettcher Hamilton Stonecroft, who had since died, leaving his fortune to Gabriel. Ezra Blackwell, his lifelong friend, chose to go with him and fulfill their common dream of exploring the west. Ezra's father was the first pastor of the Mother Bethel African Methodist Episcopal Church and Ezra had been raised by his Black Irish Mother and his firm-handed father in the ways of the Bible. But he could not be kept out of the woods where he and his friend, Gabriel Stonecroft, spent many a day cavorting about and planning the typical capers of adventuresome youngsters. Ezra was a solid-built man, about five feet ten inches tall, with solid muscle that tipped the scales at a little over fourteen stone, or about two hundred pounds. He had a natural skill with weapons and fists and counted loyalty as his best trait.

When they left Philadelphia, Gabriel's father had equipped them with the latest and best weapons, giving Gabe the rare Ferguson Rifle and a matched pair of French double-barreled pistols. He also had a turn-over double-barreled pistol by Bailes, and Ezra carried its match. Ezra had a Lancaster style flintlock rifle and later acquired a war club that had become his weapon of choice. The preferred weapon of Gabe was a Mongol bow that had a draw weight of at least a hundred fifty pounds, giving it an accurate range of over two hundred yards. Gabe had admired the weapon since his father first added it to his collection and worked hard at learning the use of it since he was big enough to draw it even a little. Gabe's father had also insisted they take a spare rifle for each and all the accouterments necessary.

The moon was waning from full and now hung low in the sky to the west. The overhead darkness was paling, and the stars were snuffing their lanterns when the two men turned to their blankets, needing some rest before they changed their travel pattern to travel the mountains in the daylight. A distant coyote sounded his plaintive cry in search of a partner, and the stone-faced mountain behind them let the morning breeze slide down its slopes to rattle the leaves of the quakies as a reminder to the two newcomers that they were not alone.

2 / Contact

The horses were tethered close by and stood hipshot, heads down, and dozing. Gabe trusted Ebony as a better watchman than himself, yet he could not sleep and rolled from the blankets and walked into the white barked aspen that stood as phantoms waving the fluttering leaves in the early morning breeze. The first light made long shadows as the sun struggled to bend its rays over and around the towering mountains. He walked through the damp leaves that packed the floor of the quaky forest, repeated wettings from morning mists made a damp mat enabling him to walk silently as he twisted his way through the trees. These times of solitude had become his moments of meditation with his God, and he treasured each one.

At the edge of the trees, he walked into the slide rock and seated himself on a large boulder. He examined the big limestone rock, noting the orange, green and grey moss that gave it the color. He lifted his eyes to the west, watching the slow painting of the hills by the gold morning light that slowly slid down the east face of the foothills. Their recent acquaintance, Francois LaRamie, a French *Coureur des Bois,* had told them of this range of mountains and about the farther range of the Wind River Mountains. He had told them these mountains they now camped in were nothing more than a teaser of the real mountains, and that made them both all the more anxious to get to the greater mountain ranges of the Rockies.

Movement caught his eye. He could barely see through the trees where the horses were tethered, and he saw Ebony lift his head and sidestep. Something was bothering him, and he was not easily disturbed. Something or someone was approaching the camp. Gabe slid from the big rock, moving at a crouch into the trees. With only his turnover pistol in his belt and a tomahawk at his side, he thought he might be at a disadvantage against any attackers and he thought, *Ain't gonna do that again!*

Two native warriors were stealthily approaching the camp. Gabe glanced to where Ezra had lain, but the blankets were empty. Ebony was sidestepping, bobbing his head, showing he was nervous and that made the other horses move. The two warriors, both with arrows nocked and their bows a partial draw, but held low, moved carefully and slowly, searching the trees for any sign of the men of the camp.

As they stepped into the clearing, one quietly spoke to the other and nodded toward the horses. Gabe knew they would try to take the animals, assuming whoever had been in the blankets were gone to the woods, perhaps hunting. They visibly relaxed and one started for the horses, but Gabe was behind the largest tree at camp's edge and stepped around just enough and threw his knife. The blade narrowly missed the face of the second warrior, burying itself in the tree trunk beside him. The warrior jumped back with a shout to his friend, and looked for the knife-thrower, lifting his bow and bringing it to full draw.

Gabe shouted, "Ho!" and held his pistol at the edge of the tree, enough for the warrior to see the muzzle of the pistol pointing directly at him. "Don't move! We mean you no harm!" said Gabe, and slowly stepped from behind the tree. He motioned for the man to lower his bow and pointed to the side where the barrel of Ezra's rifle showed alongside another tree. The two warriors had stopped in place, watching the man with the pistol and both looked at the rifle, instantly recognizing the threat. The first warrior slowly lowered his bow, releasing the draw but holding the weapon at his waist. The second warrior did the same and as they did, Gabe also lowered his pistol. But Ezra kept his rifle on them as he stepped from behind the tree but stayed in the shadows.

Gabe asked, "Do you speak English?" but the two men looked questioningly at Gabe then at one another. He asked about French and Spanish but received no response. He jammed the pistol in his belt and began to use sign, "We are friends. I am Gabe, this," nodding to Ezra, "is Ezra. We have come to trade. Is your village near?"

The first warrior relaxed, replaced the arrow in his quiver

and stood the bow at his side to use both hands to make sign and answered, speaking as he signed, "We are Hinono'eino, the Beesowuunenno' or Brush Hut people. I am Three Toes, this is Many Feathers. You are traders?"

"Yes, we have some goods to trade. But we are here to make friends with your people."

Both warriors looked with frowns at Gabe, giving little attention to Ezra who stood behind them. They looked at the stack of packs and gear beside the horses and back at Gabe, and Three Toes signed, "We would see these trade goods."

Gabe glanced at Ezra, nodded, and walked to the packs. He opened the paniers with the trade goods and brought out a couple knives, some bells, a packet of beads, and held the pack open for the men to see there were other items inside. Many Feathers looked at Gabe's tunic, noticed the bead work at the yoke and spoke to Three Toes, pointing to the beading. Three Toes asked with a scowl, "Your shirt has work of the Pawnee, did you trade with our enemy?"

Gabe frowned, then answered, "I took this off a Pawnee," knowing the implication would be that he had taken it from a dead man killed in battle, but he had traded a Pawnee woman for her work in making the tunic.

Three Toes nodded approvingly, turned to his friend and spoke in the Arapaho tongue. He turned back to Gabe, "We will tell our people of you. If our chief approves, we will return to take you to our village."

"Good. We will watch for you." He pointed to the sun and asked, "How soon will you return?"

Three Toes lifted his arm and pointed to the sun, moved his hand directly overhead and said, "There," indicating mid-day. Gabe nodded, understanding, and stepped back to let the men leave. As they turned, Ezra stepped into the light and both men stopped and stared. They stepped back away from the man coming from the shadows, eyes wide, almost in fear and looked at one another and back at Gabe. When they turned back to Ezra, he was well into the light and the two spoke to one another, looking furtively at Ezra.

Ezra chuckled, "I'm thinkin' they ain't never seen a black man."

"I think you're right," answered Gabe.

Three Toes asked Gabe, "Why is this man like the buffalo?"

Gabe glanced at Ezra, saw he was without his hat and his thick hair was somewhat ruffled and he chuckled, "He is the brother of the buffalo and he is called Black Buffalo!"

"Aiieee," cried both men as they walked quickly from the clearing, glancing repeatedly at Ezra and Gabe.

When they were gone, Gabe laughed and Ezra asked, "What'd you say?"

"I said you are the brother of the buffalo and you are called Black Buffalo!"

"Look, just cuz them Osage called me that, don't mean you can!" he feigned outrage, then chuckled, "But I do kinda like it! I think it gives me stature among the natives, don't you?"

"Oh, I'm sure. They read a lot into the name of a man. You're probably right, but just don't go wallowing in the dirt like them bulls do!"

Both men had a good laugh and knowing their time of rest was not to be, they started fixing some stew with the smoked meat and fresh Timpsila or what some called prairie turnips. But the most important part of any mealtime was the rapidly diminishing supply of coffee. They were determined to enjoy it while they had it, and Gabe filled the pot and sat it by the fire.

"Soon's we're done eatin', I think we need to move our camp. If the chief doesn't like us bein' here, they might come with not-so-friendly intentions and I'd just as soon not be here. We can find a place where we can watch from and if it's only Three Toes and Many Feathers, we can meet up with 'em and go to the village. What say you?" asked Gabe.

"You're right. I'd hate to lose this buffalo fur," rubbing his head, "to some scalping knife. I've kinda become attached to it."

They moved about a half mile across the gulch from their previous camp, and Gabe lay stretched out on a flat rock that rested on a promontory of the smaller hill. He looked straight up the draw where the two men had ridden as they left for their village. He lifted his hand to signal Ezra he had spotted someone coming. Three riders, the one in the lead was Three Toes, but the other two were unfamiliar. Gabe scowled, crawled back toward his friend, sat up and said, "There's three, but one is Three Toes." He shook his head, turned for another glance up the draw and back to Ezra,

"How 'bout you stay here with the pack horses, and I'll go down and meet them. Cover me with your rifle, just in case."

Gabe sat astride his big black, knowing the animal was impressive with his long flowing mane and tail, and when he strutted he arched his neck and tucked his chin back toward his chest and lifted his hocks in a prance, but now he stood, his stance almost daring anyone to try to get past him. Gabe left his rifle in the scabbard but was confident with his two saddle pistols holstered by the pommel and his turnover in his belt. He rested his hands on the pommel and leaned forward as the three approached.

As they neared, he frowned when he noticed one of the three was a woman, and she had pushed her mount forward of the others and spoke to him in Spanish, "You are a trader?"

"I have goods to trade, but my friend and I are just passing through, learning about the people of this land and about the country."

The woman lifted her head slightly, "Three Toes said you have many goods. Do you have rifles to trade?"

"We have rifles, but not to trade. We need them to hunt and to defend ourselves."

"They said the other man is like the buffalo, where is he?" she asked.

"He is back there," nodding his head to his left shoulder, "If you want to trade and are peaceful, we will come with you."

"We will trade."

Gabe waved his arm overhead, signaling Ezra to join

them. Within moments the clatter of hooves told of his coming from the hillside, leading the packhorses. Gabe watched the woman to see her reaction to Ezra and as her eyes flared, he let a bit of a smile paint his face. It was always interesting to see the reaction of anyone that had never seen a black man and she was no different. But she tried to remain stoic and reined around to lead them back to the village. *This should be interesting,* thought Gabe.

3 / Trade

The narrow draw followed the south face of the granite tipped peak, the tallest in the mountain range, and carried a stream that was no more than two feet wide. Often cascading over the rocky creek bed, it chuckled on its way eastward, and like most runoff streams, it followed the course of least resistance, winding its way down the rocky slope of the mountain. The game trail they followed, paralleled the stream and twisted through willows, chokecherries, and buffalo berry bushes. The trail moved away from the creek bottom and rose over a bald shoulder, made a dip between ridges then crossed a saddle to reveal a beautiful valley that stretched over a mile and half wide and five miles north and south. In the bottom was a line of green that followed a runoff creek to lower climes.

The scattered grasses had already lost their green and waved light brown stalks at the new arrivals. Gabe reined up to survey the scene before him. Scattered in the bottom near the stream were thirty plus tipis, all with entries facing the rising sun but arranged in an orderly fashion. Clusters gathered in circles around a central area in the middle of the village. Lazy tendrils of smoke rose from cookfires near every lodge. A sizeable herd of horses grazed in the upper end of the valley, watched over by several young men and boys. Children played throughout the village, some chasing hoops, others practicing with small bows and blunt tip arrows, girls sat in a circle with some game in the midst. It was a tranquil scene, not unlike any that would be found in small villages among the settlers in the east.

Gabe looked at Black Eagle and asked, "Do you have a family?"

She frowned at him, "My father is the headman of the village, and my mother is his only wife. There are no others in our family."

"No, I mean you. Do you have a man or children?"

She frowned, taking a deep breath that lifted her shoulders, turned away and said, "We will trade," ignoring his question completely.

Gabe shrugged and gigged Ebony to follow the woman warrior. He had noticed she was a very beautiful woman, at least when she wasn't scowling at him. Her long hair shone with the sunlight as it hung down her back just past her waist. She had a headband decorated with colored quills and a metallic medallion that held orange tufts of rabbit fur that dangled on different lengths of thin braided rawhide. Two feathers leaned slightly to the right and showed notches purposefully cut in a pattern. Her dark eyes blazed with wisdom and secrecy and the tiny wrinkles at the edge showed she smiled often, just not with him. Her tunic showed minimal decoration, but a thin line of yellow and red quills marked the yoke across her breasts. Fringe dangled from the yoke and down each sleeve and her leggings were tucked into the high tops of her moccasins. Her figure filled out the tunic in all the right places and try as she might to show the stoicism of a fierce warrior, her beauty spoke of character and mystery.

As they rode into the village, people watched, children followed, and some walked to the central area to see what was happening. Standing before a lodge that appeared a little larger than most was a dignified figure, greying hair in braids that hung over his shoulders, arms folded across his chest and a blanket over one shoulder and draping to the ground. Beside him a woman with wrinkled features but a smiling countenance also showed greying hair that hung loosely down her back and wearing a fringed dress that hung mid-calf. Black Eagle reined up and slipped down to stand before the man, "Father," and with a slight turn to look at Gabe, "these are the traders Three Toes spoke about." She spoke in a language not understood by Gabe, but he guessed what was being said and waited for Black Eagle to speak to him in Spanish. She turned and said, "You may get down and meet our chief."

As both men dismounted, Gabe saw they had drawn a crowd, but he chuckled as he knew most were curious about

Ezra. They stood before the chief and Eagle spoke, "This is Standing Elk, the headman of our village, and his woman, White Calf." She turned to her father, "This is Gabe Stone, and Black Buffalo." Gabe glanced at Ezra, trying to keep from grinning but the flashing eyes of his friend gave him caution. The men nodded to the chief and Gabe used sign to say, "We are honored to be here."

The chief nodded as well but asked of Eagle in his own tongue, "Are they ready to trade?"

"Yes," she answered, to which he motioned for them to display their goods so they could begin.

At Eagle's instruction, the two men began unpacking their trade goods and displaying them on a blanket. They arranged several knives, a pair of metal blade tomahawks, an assortment of metal bells used for decoration, and many bags of colored beads. There were pins, needles, linen thread, a variety of ribbons, blankets, papers of vermillion, awls, and wampum moons. They had one pot brought for their own use, but it was too big for what they needed so it was laid with the rest of the goods. As they stepped back, the chief and Black Eagle came near to examine the assortment. White Calf went immediately to the big pot and chattered and pointed, looking at Standing Elk as if demanding he trade for the item. He looked at all the items, watching his woman stay near the pot but still look at the other goods, then he walked to Gabe, and using sign, asked what he wanted for the pot.

"What do you have to trade?"

"Buffalo robe, scalps, eagle feathers . . ." he shrugged his shoulders as he looked to Gabe.

When all was said and done, White Calf had her pot, the chief had a pair of new knives, and many others went away happy with their new gewgaws. Gabe and Ezra had made deals with some women for new buckskins and moccasins, and Gabe contracted with Three Toes and his brother to make several arrows, longer than their usual and with the supplied metal arrowheads, for the Mongol bow. They had not brought out all their goods and still had ample for more trades, but they wanted to save those for other tribes.

It would take a few days for the women to make the buckskins and the men the arrows. Gabe and Ezra were invited to stay in the village and were offered a lodge for their use. Two women, sisters, were tasked with cooking for the men and when they appeared at the lodge, it was evident they were interested in Ezra, focusing all their attention on him. The older of the two appeared to be about sixteen and the other maybe two years her junior. Both were quite attractive and had their hair braided with bright red ribbon garnered in the trade. With fringed dresses and quill decorated moccasins, they stood smiling, hands clasped behind their backs, and looked to Ezra for instruction. He was as well versed in sign as was Gabe and asked, "Are you here to cook for us?"

They smiled broadly, nodded, and looked on as Ezra went to the packs and brought out a satchel full of smoked meat, the coffee pot and some coffee beans. They looked at the pot and back to Ezra, confusion showing, and he signed, "I'll take care of that. Here's some meat you can use."

They accepted the proffered meat, picked up a parfleche they brought and turned to the fire ring to start the meal. Ezra looked to Gabe, "I could get used to this," grinning widely.

"You might wanna wait until you try their cooking before you decide," suggested Gabe, prompting a frown from his friend. Ezra looked from him to the women and said, "You don't suppose . . ."

"Well, we haven't had one that couldn't cook, so far, but they are kinda young."

Black Eagle approached and looked to Gabe, "I will show you around the village," she said, as much of an order as a question, but Gabe nodded and rose to stand, motioning for her to lead the way.

As they walked, she explained, "Although we are the *Bee-sowuunenno'* or the Brush Hut people, most of our families prefer the buffalo hide tipi. When we are in our winter camp, some make the brush huts, but most use the tipi."

"Do your people move around much?" asked Gabe.

"Two times, we follow the seasons. In the time of snows, we go lower, to more protected places. But when green-up comes, we go to the mountains, like here. Because game is scarce, we might move again to where the animals are plentiful. The buffalo did not come, and our stores of meat are empty."

"Has that happened before, I mean, the buffalo not coming north?"

"Never in my lifetime. Our people depend on the buffalo for most everything. Without the migration of the herds, we might not survive the winter," Eagle dropped her head as they walked, she was obviously very concerned as well she should be, but the thought of their entire village starving was hard for Gabe to comprehend.

"Surely there are other animals that can provide meat for your people. What about elk and deer and the pronghorn?"

"The dry land has driven all away. We have taken deer, the elk are higher and far away, and the pronghorn are difficult to take. They are too fast, and it is hard to approach them, and they have so little meat. Only two of our hunters have rifles, and they are not much help, the noise drives the others away."

They continued their walk around the village, asking and answering questions, and Gabe asked about the families. "I notice each cookfire seems to have more than one woman, are they all mother/daughters or just sharing the cooking, or what?"

Black Eagle giggled, which surprised Gabe, but she explained, "No. Many of our warriors have more than one wife, often sisters, but each woman has her own lodge. The lodges and most of the things within, belong to the women. The men have their horses and their weapons, but most everything else belongs to the woman."

Gabe thought about that for a while, remembering he had seen matriarchal societies among other tribal groups, but hadn't thought about it here. He looked at Black Eagle, "You are a warrior and a war leader, can you have more than one husband?"

She laughed as she looked at him and answered, "No. One is more than enough!" she put her hand to her mouth, giggling again. Then she added, "If I take a man, I will be his only woman!"

Gabe chuckled, "Yeah, I reckon you'd be more than enough woman for any man!"

She scowled at him, then began to laugh as she realized he had expressed much the same thing as she had regarding one man/one-woman unions. She looked at Gabe and asked, "Do you have a woman?"

He shook his head at the age-old question, "No, I haven't met that one woman that would be enough for me!"

As they neared the lodge of the men, Black Eagle asked, "You have Three Toes making you arrows that are much longer than ours, but I have not seen a bow. Will you be trading for a bow?"

"No, I have my own. I keep it in a case to protect it."

"Why do you use such long arrows?"

"The bow I use has a long draw," he demonstrated the length of the draw by mimicking holding a bow and bringing it to full draw, "and shoots the arrows great distances."

She frowned, "Great distances?"

Gabe chuckled, lifted his eyes to hers, "I'll show you one day before I leave. Maybe we should go hunting. How 'bout we go after the big horn sheep up on the mountain? We saw some when we crossed." As he spoke, he pointed to the tallest of the granite peaks that stood above the camp.

She looked at him, trying to discern if he was truthful, then answered, "At first light."

Gabe grinned, nodded, "I'll be ready."

4 / Hunt

Black Eagle didn't know exactly what she expected, except that no man she had known had lived up to her expectations. This white man with the hair the color of summer's dry grass was taller than most men she knew and moved with a strength and confidence seldom seen among those of her people. He showed concern, surprise, and happiness with his eyes, and spoke easily with her. So many of those of her people were afraid of her. From the time of her youth, she had always excelled in the games used to train the young people about hunting and warfare and more often than not defeated the boys at their own games. Now as war leader, the men were more intimidated by her, as much by her position as by her abilities. She knew she was a beautiful woman and that made her the envy of the women of her tribe and to be a warrior and leader set her apart. But all that had also made her a lonely woman.

When she led her horse between the lodges toward the

tipi of the men, she was surprised to see the white man standing beside his big black horse, a packhorse nearby, and waiting for her. The first light of morning had yet to show and she thought this man and his friend would still be in their blankets, but there he was, standing with his arm under the neck of his horse, stroking the stallion's neck and talking to him. She had admired the horse as much as the man and they seemed to be an inseparable pair, each complementing the other.

Gabe saw her coming, smiled and lifted a hand in greeting. When she came near, he swung aboard his horse and nodded to her. She hopped, lay across her saddle, swung a leg over the mount's rump and sat up, reins in hand and motioned for him to lead off. The two hunters left the village quietly and Gabe pointed Ebony to the trail that came from the face of the big mountain. As they crossed the valley and started up the slope, he turned and looked at Eagle and said, "We'll go to where we saw the sheep yesterday morning. You know this country better than I do, so once we're there, I'll follow your lead."

She nodded her head in agreement as Gabe turned back to eye the trail. The first hint of light showed behind them and the mountain before them loomed large in the dim grey. The little creek gurgled over the rocks but it was smaller here. It was spring fed, the water coming from the deep underground reservoirs fed by snow melt and offered the cold water to the residents of the high mountains, often pooling in backwaters to give the animals a familiar tank for their morning and evening sustenance.

Gabe reined up and stepped down. They were on the east side of a rocky knoll and the willows beside the creek were tall enough to tether the horses. The creek bank offered green grass for their graze and Gabe spoke softly, "Where we saw them is just around this bend. The hillside is steeper and heavy with rocks, we'll make better progress afoot." He slipped the beaded leather case from under the fender of the saddle, took the quiver from the cantle, and withdrew the Mongol bow. Eagle had dismounted and slipped the unstrung bow from the quiver at her back and began to string it, watching Gabe do the same with his bow. She frowned when she saw the unusual weapon, the limbs bent back upon themselves and thicker through the grip. Gabe hung his quiver at his side, nocked an arrow and looked to Eagle to lead the way.

She nodded and walked past him, choosing to follow the small creek around the shoulder of the knoll. She paused mid-stride, lifted her free hand, and motioned before her. Gabe slowly stepped to her side to see several big-horn sheep taking their morning water. They were about sixty yards away, undisturbed and enjoying the morning. The lambs were jumping around, butting one another, as the adults took their drinks. Gabe counted four nice rams, six ewes and four lambs. He touched Eagle on the shoulder, motioned for them to back away and both slowly moved behind the stony shoulder.

He whispered and pointed above them at the far edge of

the rocky knoll. "I'll go up there, give me a few minutes to get in place, you approach from here. I'll wait until they start up the hill or until you take a shot, before I do."

Eagle frowned at him, "They are too far away! We cannot take them without being seen!"

Gabe grinned, "If you can get closer to take a shot, do it. Otherwise, I'll wait for them to start back up the mountain."

Eagle shook her head, thinking this white man knows nothing about these sheep of the mountains. No one can take a shot that far! She turned away to try to get closer to take a realistic shot, but she would wait to give him time to get over the ridge.

Gabe started up the steep rocky slope, often having to use his free hand to maneuver. The thin mountain air soon took its toll on the flatlander and he stopped, stood up and with chest heaving, sucked in the cold air as he looked back at the grey line across the eastern sky. The gold and orange showed the soon arrival of old sol and Gabe turned back to resume his climb. Although his route was no more than five hundred yards, it was steep and rocky, and it took him a while. When he reached his chosen promontory, he sat down, still breathing heavily, and looked below to see the sheep starting back up the hillside. They were taking their time and the rambunctious lambs were jumping around and playfully butting their mothers. The rams were at the back of the strung-out bunch, the ewes leading the way, and nothing showed they were alarmed by anything.

Gabe stepped beside a large boulder, hugging close so as

not to give himself away, and picked his target. The lead ewe, apparently one of the two without a lamb, picked a familiar route that zig-zagged up the steep terrain. Often jumping from one precarious spot to another, the sure-footed animals never missed a step, even the lambs jumped about as if they were in a flatland schoolyard, not a care about anything, looking as if they were smiling and laughing all the while.

He spotted the other single ewe, then chose his first target among the rams. Choosing to leave the biggest, and probably the only breeding ram of the bunch, he focused on the two younger rams, neither with close to a full curl on their horns. They were about a hundred yards distant when he stepped away from the rock and brought the bow to full draw. He took his sight and let the arrow fly. While it was still in flight, he reached to his side to pick another arrow, never taking his eyes from the soaring missile and the target.

When the arrow struck true, it took the ram in the chest, just behind his front leg, and the sheep stumbled, tried to catch his footing, but fell to the side and slid backwards down the slope about five yards, kicking as it slid. The fall of the one ram startled the others, but with no noise or appearance of any danger, they paused as they searched for the source. It was that pause that cost the second ram its life as the second arrow from the Mongol bow buried itself in its neck, dropping it to its chest, and with one last kick it breathed its last.

The rest of the herd scampered as if they heard a thunderclap, their hooves clattering across the rocks and showing only their pale rumps, they soon disappeared up the mountain. Gabe stood and started toward the downed rams, looked below him and saw Eagle starting to climb up the slope toward him. He waved and went to the second ram that was highest up the slope, knelt beside it to ensure it was dead and rolled it to its back to begin dressing it out. Eagle had stopped beside the lower ram and looked at Gabe, then looked back to where she saw him standing and shielded her eyes from the morning sun, looking back and forth from the rams to his promontory. She finally shook her head and began dressing out the ram at her feet.

They dragged the carcasses down the steep slope, which was easy enough, the only difficulty was staying out of the way and were soon beside the horses. All horses are skittish at the smell of blood, but the assuring voices of their riders calmed their concerns and they easily loaded both carcasses on the packhorse, tied them down and mounted up to return to the village. Eagle had been silent all the while, but once mounted she looked at Gabe, "One maybe, but two?" she shook her head. "You were by the big rock and that was two times farther than anyone would try to take an animal with a bow, and you took two! No misses!"

Gabe grinned, "Believe me now when I say my bow shoots great distances?"

She let a slow smile cross her face, the first he had seen, and he liked it. "Yes," she answered simply. "I would like to shoot that bow."

"You can try when we get back to the village. We'll set up some targets and see what you can do."

She rose up on her toes and leaned toward Gabe, scowling, "I am one of the best in our village! I do not miss!" she declared indignantly.

"Oh, I didn't say you would miss. It is just that it takes a lot to draw this bow to the full arrow length. Not many can do that!"

"I can do anything a man can do!" she spat. This was a constant battle she fought with herself and the many warriors of her people. She breathed heavily, her breasts rising beneath her tunic, and she sat straight in her saddle, proudly remembering her many accomplishments that proved her the equal and better of the men in her village and more.

Gabe chuckled, "We'll see, we'll see."

When they rode back into the village, many gathered around, touching the carcasses of the rams, looking at the horns, chattering about the kills. It was unusual for anyone to take a bighorn, as elusive as they are, and to bring two in was especially rare. There was much talk among the bystanders, asking Black Eagle questions, but Gabe saw her glare and countenance when she told the others that both were taken by the white man, and many looked back at him and fell silent.

Eagle asked, "What do you want to do with these?" motioning to the carcasses.

"Share 'em, of course. But I would like a couple steaks if there's any left. And I heard the hides make nice leather. Are there any women that could do that?"

Eagle nodded, barked orders to several of the women and

within moments the carcasses were taken and hung up to be skinned and distributed. Gabe grinned, stepped down and when a young man offered to take his horse, he handed off the reins and sat down near the cookfire tended by the sisters. Black Eagle had followed the group with the rams, but he hoped she would soon return. He was certain she would, as she wanted to have a try at the Mongol bow, the thought of which brought a smile to Gabe as he reached for the coffee pot.

5 / Revelation

The two friends sat near the fire, enjoying the coffee after the mid-day meal. Ezra looked at Gabe, who was sitting in a moment of remembrance grinning, and asked, "You still thinkin' 'bout Black Eagle?"

Gabe looked at Ezra, "We both know how hard it is to get a woman to go silent, but she almost bit her tongue. She wanted to say something so badly, but she just couldn't believe what she saw!"

"Didn't you say she wanted to shoot that bow?" asked Ezra, taking a long draught of the steaming coffee.

"Yeah, she did. But when I said she might not be able to, she 'bout jumped down my throat sayin' she could do anything a man could do!" he chuckled as he remembered her glaring expression when she verbally pounced on him.

"Well, looks like she's gonna take you up on that offer. Here she comes!" Ezra nodded toward the central compound where a handful of people, led by Eagle, were coming toward them. Gabe stood as they neared, still holding his coffee and lifted the cup to his lips for another sip. He smiled when he lowered the cup as Eagle stood, hands on hips, her quiver of arrows behind her back held her unstrung bow as she said, "We have set up some targets. You said I could shoot your bow. I will do that now."

Gabe looked at Ezra who slowly stood and back to Black Eagle. Beside her stood Three Toes and Many Feathers, and other warriors behind them. The group numbered only seven or eight, and Gabe asked, "Anybody else shooting?"

They looked at one another and Black Eagle translated, but after a little laughter and talking, no one answered. She looked at Gabe, "No. Just you and me."

"All right then," he said as he picked up the bow case and quiver to follow her and the group. At the edge of the village, more waited, including the chief and his woman, and other elders. Apparently, there was no one that had not heard about the feat of the white man taking two rams with his bow and at an unbelievable distance. Now, they wanted to see for themselves.

When they reached the place selected, there was a big log that marked the position for the shooters and Gabe sat down, slowly removing the Mongol bow from the case. He knew it would appear quite strange to the Arapaho, for when the bow is unstrung, its limbs are relaxed and the entire weapon makes the same shape as a man's hand as it is held, ready to grip something, or what those that knew the letters of the white man's language, a 'C'. He placed the thin woven horse-hide string loop on one limb nock, put the handle at his feet and with one foot on either side of the grip, he pulled back on the limbs to bend them back towards him bringing them close enough to place the string in the other nock.

There was considerable babble among the people as they had never seen a bow such as this nor seen anyone have to go to such measure to string a bow. Several warriors were pointing and talking, shaking their head in consternation. Gabe chuckled, stood, and nocked an arrow. He looked at the targets, two hoops with buckskin stretched across them and standing about forty yards out. He turned to Eagle, "You shoot your bow first, then you can try this one."

She nodded, lifted her bow with a nocked arrow and quickly sighted and sent the arrow whispering to its mark, hitting the target almost dead center. The crowd behind talked, laughed, and chattered. Gabe handed her his bow with an arrow nocked, said nothing but stood back to watch. She smiled as she looked at the workmanship on the weapon, felt the grip, grinned and looked at Gabe approvingly. She lifted the bow, started to draw, but the tautness of the string caused her fingers to slip off and the arrow fluttered to the ground. She frowned and looked back at Gabe who stood indifferent, watching.

She picked up the arrow, nocked it, lifted the bow and curling her fingers tightly, tried to draw the string back, bringing it about five inches back before she had to release it and again the arrow fluttered away, only this time it traveled about fifteen feet before falling to the ground. A collective gasp came from the crowd as they looked wide-eyed at their war leader. Other warriors cried out, and even though Gabe didn't understand the language, he understood the intent.

He shook his head and stepped forward to take the bow from Eagle. She looked at him, frowning, but saying nothing, as she surrendered the bow to Gabe. He looked at Ezra, "How 'bout you takin' that target out a little ways for me?" Ezra grinned, nodded and trotted to the target and carried about a hundred yards further. He drove the sticks in the ground and trotted back to the crowd. As he passed Gabe he grinned and mumbled, "Show-off!"

Gabe chuckled, and with his jade thumb ring in place, he put his thumb in front of the string, wrapped his three fingers over the thumb, then began his draw. He pulled it to full draw, took a quick sight along the arrow and let the missile fly. With just a slight arch to the flight, the arrow sped on its way and pierced the target, going through the buckskin and burying itself in the grass beyond. The entire crowd seemed frozen for just a moment, then pandemonium broke out as the people shouted and chattered and looked with wide eyes at this white man that did the impossible. The chief walked up beside Gabe and held out his hand to look at the bow. Gabe handed it to the chief and the man admired the beautiful weapon, fingering the layer of horn on the forepart of the limbs, the laminated woods, and the inlaid work of mother of pearl. It was a magnificent piece of art as well as an unbelievably deadly weapon. The chief lifted it, tested the pull and made a surprised expression, saying something to

Black Eagle in their language and Eagle grinned and nodded, looking at Gabe with greater appreciation and respect.

The chief turned back to Black Eagle, and with a hint of a grin, he spoke in the language of the people, "I believe you have found someone who is more of a man than you are a woman!"

Eagle dropped her head and did not respond, but though no one could see, she was smiling.

The sisters walked beside Ezra, but Gabe walked alone as they returned to the lodge. It was a combination of his intimidating presence, the language barrier, and the sheer shock of it all that kept everyone at a distance from Gabe, but Black Eagle came alongside and said, "They are calling you the white-man-with-the-shoots-far-bow."

Gabe chuckled, "Well, it's not as impressive as Black Buffalo, or even Black Eagle, but I guess I don't have much to say about it."

"My father has asked you and Black Buffalo to come to their lodge for a meal. White Calf and I will prepare some fresh meat from the rams for the meal, if you will come."

"Of course we'll come. It is a great honor to take a meal with the chief," replied Gabe. "We'll check on our horses first, then we'll be right along."

Eagle smiled, dropped her eyes and glanced back coyly and said, "Good," and left his side.

6 / Invitation

"So, *we* have an invitation to have dinner at the chief's lodge? But what you really mean is that *you* have an invitation to 'meet the parents' and you want me along, is that right?" asked Ezra, doing his best to keep a straight face, but failing. He chuckled as he waited for Gabe to answer.

"No, it's not that at all. I think the chief is just being hospitable and he's curious about the bow and such," replied Gabe, not being very convincing.

"Let me ask you this, is Black Eagle and her mother cooking?" inquired Ezra, head cocked to the side as he looked up at his friend.

"Yeah. So?"

"See, they want you to know she's a good cook and a good woman, not just a great warrior. Nobody wants to marry a warrior. But a good cook? That's different!"

The two men were walking to the horse herd to check on their animals, and Gabe stopped and turned to look at his friend. "Nooo, it can't be that!" he declared and started walking again.

"Then why did you bring your shaving gear?" asked Ezra, chuckling again.

"Oh, shut up!" snorted Gabe as he stomped toward the herd.

Gabe had often been admonished by his father that a true gentleman was always well groomed, regardless of the circumstances. He would recall times when he was in the Revolutionary War and always made it a point to be clean shaven, and neat and tidy in his appearance, often to the dismay of his fellow officers. Gabe had developed the same habit. Even on their travels in the wilderness, he just wasn't comfortable with stubble and shaved as often as possible. Now as he looked at his reflection in the still water of the bankside pool of the creek, he finished the last of his fastidious preparations and stood, looking at Ezra who lay back against a tree trunk, watching.

"You know, it wouldn't hurt you to at least trim those whiskers of yours!" declared Gabe.

"But the sisters like my beard!" responded Ezra, standing and brushing himself off.

Gabe looked at Ezra as they started back to the village, "Just what are their names, anyway?"

"The sisters?" he asked, receiving a nod from Gabe. "The older one is *touueekexookee* or Bobcat. The younger one is *nooku nihikoohu,* or Rabbit that Runs or something like that."

"Sounds like you're learning the language already."

"I've been learning a little. But it's not an easy language, it'll take a while."

The western mountains cradled the sun as if to impede its setting and give a few more moments to the day, but the golden orb sent lances of gold and orange to paint the underbellies of the low clouds. The brilliance gave the entire valley and the western faces of the mountains a colorful glow that showed as the Creator's last splash of color for the day. Sitting Elk nodded to the sunset, "*Be:he:eiht* honors us with His painting." He spoke in the language of the people and Eagle stepped behind Gabe and translated, "The Creator honors us with His painting, the sunset."

Gabe had been given a seat of honor to the left of the chief. Three others, elders, were seated to his right and Ezra to the left of Gabe. He learned from Eagle that the elders were part of the society of "Water Sprinkling Old Men" who were the spiritual leaders of the village. All were seated in a semi-circle around and well back from the cookfire, tended to by White Calf and Black Eagle.

Gabe had noticed the different attire worn by Eagle. She had donned a beautifully decorated, long pale buckskin dress that reached mid-calf. The entire yoke, front and back was covered with dyed quills in a geometric pattern that resembled the rising sun. Her high-topped moccasins were decorated with a similar pattern and the fringe that hung from the abbreviated sleeves, yoke, and hem of the dress held tufted feathers and bits of rabbit fur. She wore a decorated headband with similar bits of fringe that hung at the back of her head. As she and her mother served the food, she smiled often, and Gabe found it difficult to pay attention to anyone or anything besides her.

He vaguely heard someone ask a question and Eagle frowned and nodded toward her father and Gabe turned to look and saw all the elders looking at him as if awaiting an answer. He asked, "What? I'm sorry, I didn't hear you."

The chief then asked the question again, in perfect Spanish, "Did you make the bow you used today?"

Gabe relaxed, smiled and answered, "No. That is a Mongol bow and was made by warriors of the Mongol tribe that live across the great waters."

The chief frowned, and added, "I do not know the Mongol. Can you make a bow like the one you used?"

"Yes. My father and I made one, but it takes a long time and things we do not have."

"What?" he asked, meaning what things.

"There are several layers to the limbs of the bow. The outside is of horn, like the ram's horn. But the wood is different than any we have here, and the glue that holds the layers together is from a fish that is only found in the great waters. The laminating or layering" he tried unsuccessfully to demonstrate with his hands, "and the bending and gluing of the wood takes many months, sometimes more than a year, to complete."

The chief nodded, paused as if thinking on the discussion then turned back to Gabe, "Eagle says you travel at night.

How do you do this?"

Gabe smiled, lifted his eyes to the night sky and the stars that were just making themselves seen in the early darkness. He saw the Ursa Major constellation, pointed it out, "The Great Bear points the way to the north star." He pointed across the sky to the bright star, "And from the north star, we can keep our direction and know where we're going, even if we've never been there before." He looked back at the chief who let a bit of a smile tug at the corner of his face giving Gabe the impression this was not new to the chief but more of a 'let's see if this white man knows anything' kind of question. Gabe smiled, dropped his eyes to the ground and turned to Ezra, exchanging glances they both understood.

The muted thunder of hooves brought everyone's eyes up and seeing two riders coming at a run into the village and shouting, everyone stood. The horses were sliding to a stop, the men coming off their mounts before they stopped and hollered as they came near, *"Heneecee! Heneecee!"* Gabe looked to Black Eagle who was very excited and mouthed, "Buffalo!"

The chief motioned for the two scouts to calm down and explain. As Eagle told Gabe later, the men were scouts, several having been sent, that were searching for any sign of buffalo. Since the herds had not come north with the green-up, they had been sent to find them. And now these had returned with the good news. News that rapidly spread through the entire village and brought everyone from their lodges and an impromptu celebratory dance began. Eagle explained to Gabe, "This dance is an expression of thanks to the Creator for bringing the buffalo back."

"Just where are the buffalo?" asked Ezra, looking to Eagle for the answer.

"Three days south, where the river comes from the Medicine Bow mountains."

"So, your hunters are going soon?" asked Gabe.

Eagle frowned at the white man, and answered, "Our village will go. To take many buffalo will take all our people, and we need to take many for the season of snow will come soon and we need much meat." She scowled at the two friends as if she were chastising a child, shaking her head at the lack of understanding.

"May we join you on this hunt?" asked Gabe.

"Sitting Elk has asked that you come."

"Both of us?" asked Ezra, his enthusiasm showing.

Eagle smiled, nodding, "Yes. We will be on the trail by first light."

Gabe looked at Ezra, grinning, "Then I reckon we need to be gettin' our gear around."

The men were startled awake when the sisters started packing their gear out of the lodge. The men rolled from their blankets, hurriedly gathering up their personals and stuffing the parfleches full. They snatched up their weapons and stumbled from the hide lodge, just as Bobcat started disassembling the tipi. The women motioned the men aside, using sign to tell them to fetch their horses and get their gear packed up. Rabbit That Runs asked Ezra if they could use one of the packhorses for a travois to carry the lodge covering, to which he agreed, and looked to Gabe as he shrugged his shoulders. "I figgered since we traded so much stuff off, we could kinda adjust the packs and use the chestnut to haul the travois. That's all right, ain't it?"

Gabe chuckled, "Of course. After all they've done for us, it's the least we can do. They could probably put more stuff on the sorrel if they wanted."

The men were surprised at all the activity in the village. Lodges were coming down, horses were getting packed, and everyone was busy at something to get the village on the move. By first light, Eagle and her father were at the head of the long line as they started toward the valley beyond the mountains and the river that would take them south to the Medicine Bow mountains, and hopefully a large herd of buffalo. Eagle had motioned the friends forward and as they came near, she said, "We," nodding to Gabe and Ezra, "will scout ahead, hopefully to find some game for meat. There will be other scouts, but we must find meat for our people."

"Sounds fine to me. The sisters are takin' care of the pack-horses, so we are free to do whatever we can to help," replied Gabe, looking from Eagle to Ezra, who nodded in agreement.

Eagle grinned, "It is because you have rifles, and we do not have time for a stalk as we would usually do on a hunt. If you can take them where we cannot with our bows, you will help our people."

"It will be an honor," answered Gabe.

7 / Yapudttka

"They were Arapaho scouts! If they are this far south, they are after Buffalo and the herd had just come from the place of dirt of many colors. This is what we wanted! They will bring their village and while the warriors go after the buffalo, we can raid the village and take their women!" declared *Waini Muatogoci,* Two Moons, of the *Yapudttka* Ute band.

"But our chiefs do not want to fight the Arapaho!" answered Guera Murah.

"Aiieee, they already have their women! We do not! And the women of the Brush Hut people are like the sunrise, they are good to look at, more than the women of our band!"

Guera grinned, nodding his head, eyes glazing as he thought of the beauty of the Arapaho women. He was a young man, anxious to take a woman as his own, and his friend, Waini, shared those dreams. Both had proven themselves in battle and some of the families had offered their daughters as a mate, but neither were willing to take those to their lodge as their woman. To take a captive from another tribe, especially their long-time enemies, the Arapaho, would be a mark of honor. And to have an Arapaho beauty as their woman would make their standing among their own people that much greater. They would gain a measure of respect above that of other warriors. He looked at his friend, "But we are only two, we cannot do this alone!"

Waini grinned, "Our warriors have not had a good raid since before the time of snows! Most of the warriors will be glad to come! Their knives thirst for the blood of our enemies!"

"But they will not follow us!" declared Guera.

"Paheyoo Nana will lead us. He wants another woman and he has led many raids. He is a good war leader!"

Guera looked at his friend, thinking, then agreed with a head nod, "We will talk with him!"

***

Pronghorn were plentiful, but difficult to take. Herds of twenty to a hundred or more were common, but they had exceptional eyesight and speed and were easily spooked from considerable distances. Once on the run, they moved so quickly it was impossible to overtake them on horseback. They could turn, changing directions completely, without ever slowing, seemingly laying out flat as they maneuvered in mid-flight. Gabe and Ezra soon learned to utilize the terrain and approach the herd unseen until within range for a shot, and then time their shots so both could take an animal before the entire herd disappeared faster than an eagle taking flight.

The first day out they took two antelope and three deer, but among more than a hundred people, it was little enough. With an early start on the second day, and their newly discovered skill at taking antelope, they bagged four antelope and five deer, and the cook pots were full much to the delight of the people. Eagle had also shown her prowess when she easily bagged deer whenever they were near the river and the greenery that attracted the white-tail and mule deer.

They had taken three deer early on the third day and as they dressed out the animals, Gabe asked Eagle, “You said there were other groups of scouts out, but I've never seen any bring in any meat. Are they not hunting as well?”

“No. They are scouting for sign of any of our enemies. We are coming into the territory of the Ute, and they are enemies. If the herds had come north as they normally do, we would not come into their territory, but . . .” she shrugged her shoulders as she left the thought hang between them.

“Have you fought the Ute before?” asked Ezra.

“Yes. Our warriors raid their camps for horses. They raid ours for women. They raided in the time of greening, but we fought them off and sent them running away!” she declared proudly. Then added, “They did get some of our horses, but no women!”

“Do they make them slaves? Or sell them as such?” asked Gabe.

"No. They take them for mates! Our women are beautiful, theirs are short and look like men! We are tall and make good babies!"

"Oh," replied Gabe, paying close attention to his cutting of the deer carcass, dropping the subject before he said something that might get him crosswise of this woman.

A long line of rugged scarred mountains trailed off to the south and Gabe had marveled how in the middle of the vast prairie a string of mountains seemed to rise up and march away. They stayed on the west side of the meandering river that carved its way through the flats, holding the only green that could be seen in any direction, until about mid-day the third day, off to the southwest, broad shouldered black mountains stood in irregular formation and trailed off to disappear over the south horizon. Eagle pointed to the timber covered range, "Medicine Bow Mountains."

Gabe looked, turned back to Eagle, "Why are they called Medicine Bow?"

She smiled, "There is a tree that grows there, the wood is hard and strong, but not straight. It is good for bowls, platters, and more. Some make bows, if they can find a piece straight enough. Many tribes would come to this place for the wood, but also for the bark to make a tea and to use as a red dye. The leaves and flowers are also used. Because they made medicine and bows, they called the mountains the place of medicine bow."

The river forked, with the larger of the two coming from

the mountains further south, and the people crossed the small fork, staying on the northwest side near the grassy flats watered by the overflow of the stream. The many animals took advantage of the greenery, often grabbing mouthfuls as they walked.

Gabe and company had pushed on toward the mountains, aiming for the cut that marked the valley where they would make their encampment. The river snaked its way through the flats, carving its way in a twisted fashion, leaving a trail of sand bars, gravel banks, and mud bogs. One backwater had been claimed by a gaggle of geese, while a female canvasback paddled against the current, trailing a dozen ducklings behind. A flock of prairie-chickens took to flight from the tall grass at the edge of a line of cottonwood as the three riders neared. Then Black Eagle held out her hand to stop them, leaning to the side to see around a thick cluster of alder at the stream edge. She turned back and as she swung a leg over the rump of her mount, she motioned them to get down. She walked back to stand beside Gabe and whispered, "There's a big bull moose. You will need your rifle!"

Gabe nodded, stepped around behind Ebony and extracted his rifle from the scabbard. He flipped up the frizzen, blew out the powder and put in fresh, snapped it down and lowered the hammer to half cock. He looked up at Eagle, who motioned for him to follow. Ezra trailed behind, carrying his Lancaster with a fresh load.

Keeping to the brush and trees, they quietly made their way further upstream about thirty yards, and slowly slipped down the bank, where Eagle stopped. She pointed beyond the tall stand of cattails and nodded for Gabe to take the lead. He dropped to a crouch and slowly walked on the sandbar peering through the cattails and reed grass, seeing the mass of brown beyond. Suddenly he saw the massive antlers swing side to side. The big bull had been grazing on the river bottom in a wide shallow on the inside of a dogleg bend and now lifted his head at the sound of intruders.

Gabe was certain he had been seen and stepped clear of the brush to take aim. With only an instant, he brought the rifle up, bringing it to full cock as he did and took quick aim, his only target the base of the animal's neck at the shoulder. He squeezed off the shot and the big Ferguson bucked and roared. The bull started forward, but met the bullet and stumbled to one knee, rose and swung his head side to side as he bellowed his defiance. Gabe was quickly and as calmly as possible reloading the Ferguson but called, "Ezra!"

Ezra stepped forward, bringing up his long rifle, and with only a second to aim, squeezed off his shot just as the bull started his charge. The massive antlered head dropped as the towering beast rumbled forward. Ezra's bullet, well aimed at the neck of the beast, was deflected by the flat antler as the bull bellowed. Gabe was twisting the trigger guard back to close the breech when he was lifted high by the broad antlers and launched over the back of the beast. He dropped his rifle as he tumbled end over end, catching glimpses of the back of the beast as he took flight. Ezra and Eagle had scrambled for the bank and clawed their way up the muddied slope. The bull had stopped, looking around for anything to attack. Seeing Gabe on the sandbar, he whirled around, dug at the sand with his broad hooves, lowering his head for another charge.

Gabe hit the sandbar with a bone jarring thud, but he rolled over and tried getting to his feet. He saw the butt of his rifle sticking up among the cattails but out of reach. He felt at his belt for his pistol and grasped the grip, pulling it up. He brought it to full cock, fumbled at the frizzen. making sure it was dropped, as he watched the big brown mountain of a bull lean into his charge and lunge forward. Gabe was on his feet. He feinted toward the water, then jumped to the bank side, pointing the pistol at the charging monster. He waited just an instant and fired. In that moment, he saw the puff of impact as the wet and muddy hair blossomed and the bullet penetrated the thick hide. The bull staggered slightly and slid to a stop, turning for another charge.

Gabe quickly swiveled the barrels on the pistol, cocked the hammer and stood his ground. The bull again lowered his head and began his charge. Gabe sucked air, tested his footing and readied himself. The bull was within six feet when he triggered the second round as he jumped as far to the side as he could. As he crashed into the thick cattails, he was certain he heard another blast, but he didn't understand how that was possible. He rolled over, jumped to his feet and started to run for the bank, but no sound came from behind him and he dared to look back, saw nothing, and stopped, frowning. He tiptoed just enough to see a brown heap in the shallow water at the edge of the sandbar. He stepped forward slowly, still holding the empty pistol, and looked to see the downed moose, unmoving at water's edge.

"He's down!" came a declaration from behind him. Ezra and Eagle came from the brush and walked to Gabe's side. They looked at the carcass of the big moose from a distance, then Ezra said, "I'll check him." He walked forward, pistol in hand, empty rifle in the other, and poked the beast with the muzzle of the rifle, then stood up, relaxed as he turned back to his friends. "He's dead!"

Gabe sat down on the sandbar, arched his back and felt his legs and arms, looked at his friends, "I feel like I should be dead too!"

Eagle came to his side, seated herself beside him and touched his arm that was already starting to show a big bruise. "That must have hurt. When I saw you fly, I thought it was just another white man trick," she tried to keep a straight face, but failed as the corners of her mouth drew back and her eyes showed laughter.

Ezra called out, "Didn't know you had feathers! But you sure took flight! Better'n them ducks that took off!" He laughed as he walked back to look at his friend.

"Just for that, you two get to butcher that beast!" Gabe answered. He made a face, arching his back and putting his hands to his neck. "I think I'll just rest up here on the warm sand." He scowled as he lay back, moaning in pain as he did.

8 / Encampment

Gabe was fascinated at the efficiency and order of the people as they set up their camp. He was reminded of an anthill of activity with everyone running around and no one in charge, but everything getting done and done properly. He watched as the women erected the tripod of tipi poles, then lay the rest in place before drawing the heavy hides stitched into the lodge pattern up the poles. They then inserted the flap poles and secured it together with the carved and fashioned sticks that looked like stitching on a seam. He knew the lodges would have a half-liner in the cold months, but none were added on this day. The lodges and the women were patterns of efficiency and the entire village rose and appeared as if it had been a long time here.

He and Ezra had seated themselves just inside the tree line, out of the way of those that knew what they were doing and watched as the sisters walked toward them to let them know their lodge was ready. The camp was stretched along the small creek that fed into the river the Arapaho called the River of Medicine Bow but would one day be called the Laramie. The small creek came from the west side runoff of the lone mountain that stood east of the main Medicine Bow range, and although small, it was enough to provide water for the camp and their animals. The horses were always kept downstream of the camp and would be picketed at the tree line come nightfall. Many of the hunters would bring their favorite buffalo horse to their lodge and have it ready for the pre-dawn departure, as did Gabe and Ezra.

The men were a little taken aback when they entered the lodge. On one side, several buffalo robes lay as a sleeping platform with their blankets rolled out and their parfleches nearby. But across the fire ring, was another arrangement of robes and blankets. They looked at one another and Ezra shrugged his shoulders and went outside to talk to the sisters. They were tending the cookfire and ignored the two as they came from the lodge.

Ezra asked, "Uh, who else is sleeping in the lodge?"

Both women looked up, frowning, showing their lack of understanding. Ezra repeated his question, using sign and his limited Arapaho. When they understood, the sisters smiled and pointed at themselves. Ezra looked to Gabe, "Now what?" he asked.

Gabe was more fluent with sign and said, "We cannot sleep together. We," pointing to himself and then to Rabbit, "are not mated."

Both girls sat back on their heels, laughing, prompting

confused expressions on both Ezra and Gabe. Then Bobcat explained, "We are not sleeping together. You are on one side; we are on the other. We could only bring one lodge so we must share."

"What was so funny?" asked Gabe, signing.

"You said we are not man and woman. I know you meant to say we are not a couple or husband and wife. But you are men and we are women!" she giggled as she signed.

Gabe chuckled as he looked to Ezra, "Did you catch that?"

"Ummhumm, sure did. And she's right, you know. We are men and they are women, that's the problem!" answered Ezra.

"Would you have them or us sleep outside?" asked Gabe.

"No, but . . ." he responded, shaking his head.

The massive herd was bedded down in an ancient lakebed where a half-circle of broken and scattered limestone boulders marked its southern shore. Eons of time had deposited shells and seeds that marked the basin with splotches of green and grey. Little was seen but the rumpled blanket of brown that told of the herd that would grow restless with daylight. The scouts had reported on the whereabouts, giving the chief and other leaders time to plan the hunt.

Black Eagle came to the lodge of the men to share the details for the coming day. With the evening meal just finished, Gabe and Ezra were seated on a blanket outside by the cookfire, enjoying their coffee when Eagle's face was lit by the glow as she neared. Gabe quickly stood and offered her a seat on the blanket which she accepted and when Gabe was seated, she began, "The herd is beyond that hill," pointing to the low range of hills to the southeast of their camp. "They are in a wide basin, like this," and began drawing in dirt before them. "There is a line of stone along here," making a wide semi-circle, "and you will approach from below. When you get to the top, you will shoot to cause the herd to move toward the river, here." She made a squiggly line to indicate the river they followed to their camp. "The other hunters will come from here, and here," indicating the east and west sides of the hoped-for route of the buffalo.

"Will you be there with us?" asked Gabe.

"I do not have a rifle. Only three of our warriors have rifles and they will be with you."

"I have a spare rifle if you want to come with us," suggested Gabe.

"I must lead the others. You will lead the shooters," explained Eagle.

When Gabe threw the flap back, he stuck his head out of the tipi to look at the moon and stars to gauge the time, nodded and stepped back to stir Ezra awake. "Time to go," he whispered. "It's a couple hours past midnight and it'll take all of that to get where we're supposed to be," he explained as Ezra moaned and stretched himself awake. They were tightening the girths on the horses when three warriors rode up. Gabe looked up in the waning moonlight and saw the familiar faces of Three Toes, Many Feathers and Runs Far. He nodded as he swung aboard Ebony and with a quick glance to Ezra, he looked to Three Toes and said, “Lead off!”

They moved single file around the knob of a mountain and took a tack toward the south at the edge of the wide valley. Now in the open, Gabe rode alongside Three Toes who told him of the many-colored soil at the south edge of the open plain. The moon dropped from its lofty perch and hung placidly just above the mountains to their right, west of the valley, when they came to the rock rimmed lakebed that held the buffalo. From the distance, the brown blanket of bison appeared as a low black cloud that hugged the flats. Yet the men moved further south before turning to the east and the thin line of grey at the horizon.

The rim of strewn rock rested at the edge, about a hundred feet higher and two hundred plus yards away. With signs, Gabe directed the three warriors further along the rim to the east while he and Ezra would mount it where they were, Ezra staying back to Gabe’s left. He told the three, “Keep your horses below the ridge, but once the buffalo start to move, use your mounts and keep ‘em moving.”

At first light, Gabe opened the hunt with his first shot dropping a young bull. The shots from Ezra and the three warriors came so quickly after his, they sounded as echoes. The herd came to their feet, the big bulls began pushing and the herd was on the move. They could feel the earth tremble beneath them, as the big woolies thundered away. As they scrambled to their horses, the men fumbled with their weapons, loading on the run.

The buffalo moved as one, dust rising like a storm cloud over them, dirt clods, rocks, and more kicked aside and behind them. The soil appeared as if a gang of plows had tried to turn the dry flats into farmland, tilling the soil in preparation of planting. But the only planting to be done was the offal from the slaughtered animals. The rumble of hooves was discordant with the bellowing of the beasts, bulls goading the herd on, cows calling for the calves and calves for their mothers, but most just complaining about the rude awakening.

Suddenly from both sides came bands of mounted warriors, shouting and screaming as they swung alongside the beasts. Most used bows, shooting their arrows into the flanks of the animals, causing them to stumble and give a better chance at a kill shot. Some used lances, holding the long shaft under their arms and leaning in with the charge of their mounts, driving the big point deep into the chests or necks of their targets. Big bodies often tumbled end over end, crashing down in a cloud of dust, while others stumbled, driving their chins into the hoof tilled soil and sliding to a stop.

Gabe and Ezra both scored another killing shot, and Gabe learned later that two of the three with him had also killed their chosen target. The third had a clear miss, but rode alongside a cow, and on the run, put the muzzle behind her ear and jerked his kill shot, almost losing his rifle in the process. As they chased after the herd, Gabe scored another kill shot while Ezra wounded one that stumbled, and hit from behind by another bull, rolled end over end and lay still with an obvious broken neck. Both men reined up and sat still, reloading and watching the other hunters and the stampeding buffalo.

One of the Arapaho warriors, using a bow had shot into the side of a big bull and while Gabe and Ezra watched from a distance, the bull turned, hooked the horse in the shoulder and plowed it over atop the rider. The bull butted the down horse again, tried to hook it in the neck as he passed and stomped on the chest of the warrior whose leg was trapped under the horse. Gabe finished his reloading and as he spun the trigger guard on the Ferguson to close the breech, he dug his heels into the sides of Ebony, causing the big black to lunge forward into an all-out run, heading for the downed warrior. Gabe reined up, put the powder in the flash pan, slapped it shut and eared the hammer back to full cock. He gigged Ebony into a trot to go beside the trampled man and looked up to see the big bull turning around and lowering his head for another charge. Gabe jerked the reins to the side, kicking Ebony and shouting. The big bull charged, head down so low his beard drug in the dirt, tongue lolling, eyes blazing and digging his forefeet into the soft soil, determined to take the black down. The big horse dug his heels in and lunged to the side, barely missing being gored, and kicked out at the beast as he passed. Gabe swung the rifle around, hugged it to his side and pulled the trigger.

The blast was as nothing in the pandemonium of the stampede and slaughter, but the rifle bucked, spat flame, smoke and lead, and the offhand shot slammed into the neck of the brawny beast, instantly blossoming blood and knocking the animal stumbling to the side. With no time to reload the rifle, Gabe jammed it into the scabbard beneath his right leg and in one motion snatched up the saddle pistol, cocking the hammers as he did. The red eyes of the big bull glared, his tongue dripped with slobbers and blood, and the massive head swung side to side. The bull dug at the dirt, throwing clumps behind him with each grab, then bellowed and charged. Gabe waited an instant, then fired the first barrel, then the second, the smoke following the flame and lead balls toward the charging beast, and the mass of brown meanness stumbled, dropped his head to the ground and dug a furrow in the dirt with his chin. He slid so close, Ebony reared up and back, almost unseating Gabe, but they came down together. Ebony sidestepped, neck craned around, wide eyes watching the carcass, but the calm, soothing voice of Gabe soon stilled the big animal and they both sat, watching the herd disappear in a cloud of dust.

9 / Discovery

Gabe watched as Ezra reined around and started back to where he waited. Both Ebony and Gabe were doing their best to settle down after the clash with the rampaging bull. Their sides had been heaving as they gasped for breath, hearts beating as if they wanted to escape their chests, and nerves strung tight, so tight they both shook. But as they began to relax, knowing it was over, they stood together, Gabe on the ground, his arm under and around the big black's neck as they watched Ezra come near.

Ezra looked at his friend, then at the massive bull that lay as a mound of brown, and back to Gabe, "Close one, huh?"

Gabe nodded to the horse and warrior behind them, both dead and obviously trampled, "He got this one first then turned on me. Took a bit o' doin' but there he be!"

"I wondered what got into you back there. You took off like a scared rabbit, but the dust was too thick for me to see where you went," explained Ezra, looking to his friend. "Glad you're all right!"

He started to reply but saw Black Eagle coming and watched as she drew near. She smiled, "It has been a good hunt! Our people have many buffalo!" She looked at the big bull beside them, "The big ones are tough meat. You should have taken a young one."

Gabe dropped his eyes, then looking back up at Eagle, "He didn't give me much of a choice." He stepped aside and nodded behind him. "This one," pointing to the bull, "took him down and I tried to get here but was a little late. He," nodding again toward the bull, "tried to get me and Ebony here, but we didn't cotton to that idea any."

Eagle walked back to the trampled horse and man, knelt beside them, then stood looking back at Gabe, "He was a good warrior and hunter. He has a wife and child." Gabe noticed her not referring to the man by his name, but he was familiar with the manner of many of the native people about not using the name of a dead man. Some did not for fear of bringing the spirit of the dead person back, others just out of respect. She stood and looked back toward the camp, then off to the killing grounds, and back to the river carved notch between the mountains. She frowned, "His woman," pointing back to the downed man, "and the others should be coming. They are usually here, as soon as the herd passes, to start the butchering. Perhaps something is wrong," she scowled, stepping back beside her horse.

She swung aboard and looked to Gabe and Ezra, "Come with me."

Gabe saw her concern and without questioning, both

he and Ezra mounted up and rode with her. As they rode, she waved other warriors to follow and when they entered the cut, she was trailed by more than a dozen warriors. The nearer they came to the camp, the more concerned they became. By now, all the women and children should be coming to the buffalo to tend to the carcasses and rejoice with the hunters for the great hunt. But nothing moved.

When the camp came in sight, there was more smoke than usual and they heard wailing that could only mean one thing, death had visited the village. Everyone grabbed at their weapons, men nocking arrows, Gabe and Ezra checking their loads, others brought their lances under their arms, points lowered. Eagle kicked her horse to a canter, her bow held at her side, as she leaned forward, standing in her stirrups. The rest of the men were close behind, all stretching to see. Gabe was beside Eagle as they spotted the first body, a white-haired woman impaled with a lance that had broken and the shaft lay at her side. Sightless eyes stared at the blue sky above, the hide tipi beside her now nothing but a charred stack of poles, smoke lifting into the still morning.

The group scattered, hurrying to their lodges, looking for their families. Wailing cries rose into a cacophony of sound, whinnying horses, screaming men and women, bawling babies, snapping of burning wood, angry fists hitting at lodge poles and more. There had been many women and children left behind with the old people. But now most of the bodies had grey or white hair as they had tried to defend their village. The women that remained had been wounded and left for dead or had already left this world.

Eagle rushed to the lodge of her family, and although it still stood, the flap was open and she rushed inside to see the prostrate form of her father, her mother bending over beside him. She lifted her eyes to Eagle and said, "He still lives," and leaned back so Eagle could see. Her father's chest was bloody, the shafts of two arrows still protruded, and his breathing was ragged.

She dropped to her knees beside him, looked to her mother, "Who?"

"Ute!" she snapped, wrinkling her nose in disgust and hatred.

Gabe was waiting outside the lodge when Eagle came out. She looked around, saw someone and took off at a run. She grabbed an old man by the arm and dragged him back to her lodge. She spoke in her tongue, motioning to the lodge and the man stepped inside. Eagle looked at Gabe, "He is a healer, a medicine man. My father has two arrows, here and here," she pointed at her chest. She looked around, glaring, anger showing as she scanned the camp. "I must know how many are gone!" she declared and took off at a run to move through the camp, looking in every lodge that still stood and all around the camp.

Gabe started for their lodge, having seen it still standing when they returned. Ezra had already gone to check on the sisters and when Gabe arrived, he stood before the entry, shaking his head. "They took 'em, both of 'em!" He looked up at Gabe, "We gotta go get 'em!"

"We will, but we've got to wait for Eagle, and I'm sure there will be others that want to go."

"Mebbe so, but if we go now, we can scout the trail, maybe find 'em!" he declared. Gabe looked at his friend, took a moment to think, "Let's get some food and whatever else we might need. This might take a while."

When Eagle rode up to their lodge, she was astride a muscular blue roan gelding, with dark legs, dark mane and tail, a small white diamond marked his dark face. Behind her were a dozen stern-faced warriors, and she looked at Gabe with a sneer, "You will come with us?"

"Of course. We've got our gear and we're ready." He nodded to Ezra, and both men stepped into their stirrups and swung aboard. Eagle led off and Gabe was beside her, "Who was it?" he asked.

"Ute! They took two hands and one women, three girls, and the horses."

"Fourteen women and the horses, two of which are ours. How many Ute were there?"

"Maybe three hands."

Eagle had already sent three scouts ahead and as they left the camp, she kicked her roan into a ground eating canter, everyone keeping pace, and all determined to exact revenge as well as recapture the prisoners. After a couple miles, she dropped into a trot and was soon letting her horse walk. She reined up, slid off her horse and started walking and leading the roan. The others followed her example and Gabe marveled at the discipline of the men, none objecting, all trusting and willing to follow without complaint. They covered about a mile and a half, when Eagle climbed back atop the roan and started off at a walk.

The trail of the Utes was easily seen, with so many warriors and the stolen herd, there was no way to disguise their tracks, nor did they try. It was evident they were pushing the horses hard and undoubtedly expected pursuit. But there was a limit to the stamina of the horses and not knowing how far they traveled before the attack, it was impossible to know how far they would go before camping. And there was the uncertainty of where their village was and if there would be other warriors waiting for their return.

Eagle had kicked her roan back up to a canter and the clatter of hooves from a dozen more riders racketed across the narrowing valley. The raiders were following the river upstream and the nearer they came to the headwaters, the narrower the canyon. The shadows from the surrounding mountains grew long and stretched across the green valley, but the trail led on and the Arapaho did not wane in their pursuit. The black timbered mountains shouldered closer to the river, their slopes rising steeply, and the lowering sun had difficulty sharing its light with the river bottom. Eagle had again dropped the roan back to a walk and she looked around at the mountains and the diminishing light. She looked to Gabe, "We will keep on till we can no longer see, then we will camp. The captives will be treated all right, until they get to their village. Then . . ." and she shrugged, unknowing.

Gabe guessed they had covered about twenty miles when

the canyon split, a small stream coming from a mountain valley and the river turning directly south. The trail of the raiders still followed the river, but darkness was dropping its curtain when Eagle signaled a halt. Standing beside the river, their horses beside them, were the three scouts. All had somber faces and Eagle was not pleased. As they neared, one of the scouts spoke, "They have made camp, but it is far."

Eagle stepped down and spoke with the scouts, questioning what they had found and soon came back to the others, "We will camp here. The Ute are camped, but too far to go tonight. We will talk and decide."

None of the Arapaho had brought much in the way of food, most had bags of pemmican or jerky, some with a type of biscuit or johnnycake. Gabe and Ezra were no different, choosing to travel light and fast, but Ezra had ensured they brought a good amount of pemmican and johnnycakes. He handed a couple corn cakes to Gabe, then a handful of pemmican and the men sat down to enjoy the meal, such as it was. Eagle joined them and Ezra shared their stores with her, which she happily accepted, having been too preoccupied with her father to concern herself with rations.

Gabe asked, "How was your father?"

"He will live. The shaman took out the arrows, tended his wounds and White calf will take care of him."

"Good, good," replied Gabe. "Do you plan to go further tonight?"

"No, but maybe in the morning, early, we can take them."

10 / Skirmish

It wasn't the nature of either Gabe or Ezra to sit idly by as someone else thought things out, made a plan, and expected others to follow. Both men had always been eager to take the initiative, make their own plans, and execute them promptly. Now as they sat together, considering, Gabe knew Eagle's mind was torn between concern for her father, her responsibilities as war leader, and the danger faced by the captives. Gabe leaned forward, "I'm thinkin' that if we go stormin' up on 'em, there's gonna be some of the captives hurt. They'll use 'em as shields or kill 'em outright."

Eagle twisted around to look at Gabe, "But what else can we do? There are as many of them as us," she nodded toward the others that were gathered nearby.

"Do what they don't expect. Maybe just a handful of us, 'cuz I don't think they'll wait till mornin' to leave." He lifted his eyes to the night sky, saw the moon waning to three-quarters, "We've got enough light to see, and we're not going far.

Our horses could stand a little more, we tether 'em, approach on foot. Take some of 'em out, spook the rest."

"That could make them kill the captives," replied Eagle, interested in Gabe's plan, but still concerned.

"Not if the captives are gone."

"Would you do this?" asked Eagle.

"Maybe you and two of your best men, those that are good at moving quiet-like. Ezra and I work well together, and I think we might get it done."

"This is Steals Horses and Moonwalker. They were the scouts and know where the Ute are camped," stated Eagle as they approached. Gabe and Ezra had readied themselves and sat on their horses, waiting. Gabe nodded and motioned for the scouts to lead out.

Although the bright stars and three-quarter moon provided ample light, it was a cloudy night and they often rode in the shadows. It took less than a half hour to reach the promontory above the Ute camp. They had followed the river as it twisted through the bottom of the wide canyon, but now rose up on the shoulder of a long slope that had its terminus in a dogleg of the river. Steals Horses motioned them to the ground and the group went to a crouch to mount the edge of the shoulder.

The moonlight shone on the water as the river bent around a peninsula of cottonwood, willows and chokecherries. The horse herd stood between the edge of the bald slope and the cottonwoods, while the Ute and captives were scattered in the trees and shrubs. From their location it was impossible to discern the captives from the captors, but Gabe noted three sentries, each near a gangly cottonwood. They watched and waited, studying the lay of the land and any possible approach to the encampment. At Eagle's signal, they crabbed back from the edge, worked their way back to the picketed horses and looking to one another, Gabe began, "Three sentries, they'll need to be taken first. But not knowing more about where the captives are we'll have to decide on the fly what to do."

"No," stated Eagle. "We'll take the sentries, then scatter the horses while others free the captives."

Gabe looked at her, nodded, "All right. You'll be the one to free the captives. They will know you and not be alarmed. Ezra and I will each take a sentry, one of you," nodding to the two scouts, "will take the other. While whoever's left with scatter the horses."

Eagle nodded and spoke to the scouts, "Stealer, you, horses. Moonwalker, take the other sentry."

Gabe turned to Moonwalker, "You take the scout near the river. You'll need to come from the water, but we," nodding to Ezra, "will wait for you before we take ours." Although Gabe spoke in Spanish, Eagle translated to ensure there was no misunderstanding with Moonwalker.

Gabe took to the trees that covered the slope downstream from the encampment, while the others dropped behind the shoulder, following the wide draw to the flats below. With the horse herd at the north edge of the peninsula, they had to make their way around the animals, before moving along the river shore to approach the camp.

They had just dropped below the edge of the bank when Eagle suddenly stopped, motioning the others down. She pointed ahead where a previously unseen sentry sat on a boulder in the shadow of a stunted cedar. She motioned to Steals Horses and he slipped over the edge of the bank, moving silently in the dark behind the man. As he drew near, Eagle threw a pebble to the far side of the man, catching his attention just long enough for Steals to take him from behind. Within moments, the sentry was down, and Steals dragged the body behind the boulder. He motioned the others on and took the sentry's place on the rock.

When they neared the thicker brush and cottonwoods, Eagle motioned Moonwalker to move downstream toward his target and nodded to Ezra for him to take his place. She would wait until she thought Moonwalker was in place, then would move into the trees to search out the captives. Nothing stirred, the chuckle of the river cascading over the rocks covering any sound they might make. Within moments, all three were in the trees, searching for targets and captives.

When Gabe left the others, he trotted into the trees and moved as silently as a cougar on a stalk, whispering through the scattered juniper and cedar. He glanced at the sky, saw the moon nearing a cloud bank and knew he would be in the dark soon. He nodded to himself, grinning, knowing he could see well enough to find the rock outcropping he had spotted from atop the ridge. Once to the promontory, he dropped to one knee, breathing deeply to catch his wind, and looked toward the camp. He had marked the sentry's cottonwood by the skeletal branches that stretched toward the stars, and quickly located the sentry below. He had seated himself, legs stretched out and leaning back against the gnarly trunk but appeared watchful. Yet Gabe knew a comfortable sentry was a sleepy and careless sentry and grinned at the thought.

With another glance at the clouds, he dropped off the rocks and padded toward the river's edge. Once there, he dropped down on one knee, looked toward the sentry, felt the butts of his two pistols and gripped his bow with the nocked arrow, and was reassured by their presence. Seeing no movement, Gabe started his stalk at the edge of the trees and brush, working toward his target. When he was within about thirty feet, he went to his belly, laying his bow in the grass and slipping his knife from the scabbard in his tall moccasins. He watched the guard and beyond to the camp, seeing the forms of several, stretched out and under their blankets.

With no movement from either the camp or the sentry, Gabe began to move closer. Knife in his teeth, he used his fingers and toes as he lifted himself above the grass and moved forward. When he was within about eight feet, the sentry moved, and Gabe dropped to his belly in the grass, unmoving, holding his breath, watching for any other movement. The sentry stretched, probably yawned, but with his back to the cottonwood and Gabe behind the tree, he couldn't see but just the shoulders of the man. As he grew still and his breathing was shallow and regular, Gabe rose from the grass, took two slow strides, and stepped from behind the tree, quickly putting one hand over the sentry's mouth. He slid the razor-sharp blade across the sentry's throat, prompting the man to kick out, eyes showing white, as he tried to grab Gabe's hand so he could shout a warning, but blood spilled from the maw below his chin and he slumped still in death.

Gabe knelt beside the tree, watching the camp for any movement, wiped his hands and knife in the grass, and satisfied, returned for his bow. With bow in hand, he went to a crouch and worked his way into the tree line, and toward the camp. He had spotted some sleepers that were apart from the others and determined to try to lower the odds against them. When near, he leaned the bow against a cottonwood, dropped in a crouch and began his approach. Two men lay near a cluster of willows, apart from the others, and had put their blankets in the thick grass for comfort, but their comfort would be their undoing.

With knife in hand, Gabe paused near the first man, who lay on his side, facing away from the other, and snoring lightly. Gabe stepped across the man, looked at the other, then in one quick move, dropped to one knee, driving his blade into the man's back as he stifled his cry with a hand over his mouth. The knife drove in to the hilt, and Gabe twisted the blade, drew it to the side, while he had one knee on the man's ribcage, and his hand over his mouth. With a frantic kick and flared eyes, the man breathed his last.

Gabe looked quickly to the nearest warrior, saw him stir

and with a fluid movement, he stretched across the space, and drew the knife blade across the man's throat as he reached to cover his mouth. The warrior grabbed at Gabe's hand, but was too late as the long blade split his throat open and he choked on his own blood. Gabe looked around at the other sleepers, saw some movement and dropped to his belly between the two dead men. As he lay still, he slowly lifted his head to look about the camp, saw no movement, then looked to the other sentries. Neither sentry could be seen, and Gabe searched to be certain he looked where they had been spotted. Reassured, he watched shadows move slowly toward sleeping forms and knew Moonwalker and Ezra were taking a toll.

Suddenly, the thunder of hooves told of the horse herd scattering. The camp was instantly alerted, and men threw off blankets and grabbed for weapons, looking to the trees where the horses had been herded together, but were now stampeding. None expected enemies within their camp and Gabe lunged for his bow. He spun around as he nocked an arrow and brought his weapon to full draw, sending the feathered missile toward the target of a big Ute. The arrow took him in the side, just below his armpit and dropped him to the ground. Another arrow whispered past and impaled a second warrior with such force it drove him into the back of another man, impaling them both and driving them to the ground.

As the running warriors came to the edge of the trees, they were startled when the big black man jumped from behind a tree, wielding his war club over head as he screamed his attack. Ezra had stripped off his buckskins and now clad only in a breechcloth and tall moccasins, his black skin shone in the darkness and his wide eyes flared white. His warclub whistled as he swung it in an arc over his head and stepped into his swing, bringing the sharpened halberd blade toward a startled Ute who held his expression as he was decapitated, sending the head bouncing toward those behind him. One of the Ute screamed, not a war cry but in shock and he jumped over the bouncing head and looked at this black monster that was dealing death. Ezra spun around with another swing, lunging forward with the momentum of the club and struck another warrior who lifted an arm to protect himself, and lost it as the halberd was buried in his chest. Blood squirted from the severed arm and stump. The warrior, mouth agape and sightless eyes staring, fell to the side. Ezra put his foot on the man's chest to yank his war club free and screaming, searched for another victim.

An arrow whispered past his head and Ezra searched for the shooter, but another man was charging with a lance held at his waist. Ezra feinted to the right, making the man move slightly, then Ezra spun around to his left, swinging the deadly weapon overhead and bringing it down atop the man's shoulder at his neck, crumbling him like a rag doll. Ezra snatched his warclub free, let loose a bellow that echoed from the hillside and beat on his chest as he searched for another Ute. But none were to be found. At his feet lay three dead men, just beyond three more with arrows protruding from their backs or necks, arrows he recognized as Gabe's.

A rustling in the brush behind him made him spin around, lifting the warclub high, but he stopped in mid-swing as the brush parted to show several of the captive women coming through. Two rushed toward him and he recognized the sisters just before they wrapped him in their arms, chattering away in their tongue, but refusing to let him go. He chuckled as he put his one arm around Bobcat, leaned his head atop Rabbit's and held to his warclub beside them. They were followed by Black Eagle, who stepped forward with a nocked arrow on her bow, searching the area for any threat. She saw the scattered bodies, frowned when she noticed the one without a head, then looked at Ezra, shaking her head.

11 / Revelation

"Well, look at you! Standin' out here in your all togethers, gettin' hugged on by two women, and you not even properly dressed! You oughta be ashamed!" declared Gabe, grinning at his friend. "Did the Ute try to scalp you and couldn't get a grip, so they took your clothes instead?"

Ezra dropped his eyes as he chuckled at his friend's comments, then lifted his gaze up and said, "Nope. Just bein' practical. Look at 'chu! All bloody an' such. You ain't gonna get that blood outta them buckskins, whereas myself, I'm just gonna go jump in the river yonder, and I'll be clean as a whistle! Then I'll put on my duds, an' be as handsome as ever. You, on the other hand, look like you just came from a butcher shop, all bloody an' all. Next you're gonna be tellin' us some tall tale about fightin' an' such. Didn't your mama teach you better?"

The two friends laughed and hugged one another, relieved that they were both unharmed. Gabe turned to Eagle, who stood staring at the two, mouth agape at their repartee, and asked, "All the captives all right?"

She looked at Gabe, shook her head and answered, "Yes. All are good."

"Then we gonna head on back or wait till daylight?" asked Gabe. But the sudden clatter of hooves took their attention and they turned to see Three Toes leading most of the remaining warriors toward them. He pulled up beside Eagle, slid to the ground, and reported, "Steals Horses told us about the fight. I left some men to help with the horses, they will be here soon."

"You did well," replied Eagle, then turning to Gabe, explaining, "I told him to bring the others."

Gabe nodded, "Just in case we couldn't pull it off?"

She grinned, "Yes."

It was a relieved and joyous band that returned to the encampment that morning. Not only did they rescue the captive women, but the horses as well. And they also had the extra benefit of the Ute horses, fifteen to be exact. They were awarded to the captives who gave them to their rescuers, each one considered a prize. When they returned, the survivors chose to turn their mourning into a celebration of the bountiful hunt, the recovery of the captives, the capture of the horses, and the victory over the Ute.

Gabe and Ezra, quite tired from the chase and fight, chose to get a little sleep while others prepared for the feast and the celebration. But the time of rest was cut short by the activity in the camp. There was just too much going on that aroused the curiosity of the friends. They soon rolled from their blankets and went outside to sit by the fire where the sisters chattered on about the rescue and their hero rescuer, Ezra. With a few words in Spanish, English, and sign, they made themselves understood and Ezra chuckled that he was getting all the credit as if he had rescued them singlehandedly. He looked to Gabe, "See what takin' off muh shirt did? When they saw these muscles," he flexed his biceps that showed under the loose-fitting buckskin tunic, "they just thought I done it all!"

"That all right, we both know better. But, you just enjoy this attention now. That'll just make it all the harder when we have to leave here," replied Gabe, reaching for the coffee pot.

Ezra scowled at him, "Yeah, guess so. Didn't really wanna think about that."

"So, you thinkin' 'bout settlin' down with one of the sisters?" asked Gabe.

Ezra looked at his friend, "What 'bout you an' Eagle? You two been mighty friendly lately."

Gabe sipped at his coffee, thoughtful in the moment, "She's quite a woman," he mulled. Then looking up at Ezra, "But, we've met others and will probably meet more, and, we've got plans, don't we?"

"Well, yeah, but . . ." responded Ezra, with more regret than resolve. He sat on the grey log, elbows on knees, cup held with both hands as the steam from the coffee drifted near his face, and looking at his friend, he continued, "There's times that I wonder how much better it could be with a woman by my side. One that could share in my dreams and hopes and more. One that would always stand by me, even fight alongside me, but always be with me. Then there's times when I think that taking a woman with me would be more selfish than sacrificial, and my Pa always said, *Love is self-sacrifice. God is love, and He told about that love in John 3:16, 'For God so loved the world that he gave . . .' that's self-sacrifice.*"

"Yeah, that's the same as what my Pa used to always say, *Son, love is not what you get, it's what you give!*"

Both men lapsed into a moment of introspection and contemplation as their eyes glazed over, and they sat motionless, staring into the low burning flames of the cookfire. Their reverie was interrupted by the voice of Black Eagle as she seated herself beside Gabe and said, "My father wants to see you before the feast."

"Is there something I should be concerned about?" asked Gabe.

"No, he has a gift and an honor for you. He is grateful, as we all are, for what you and Black Buffalo have done for our people."

Gabe slowly nodded, looking at Eagle, who smiled, but Gabe detected a bit of mischievousness in her manner and expression. He squinted as he looked at her and asked, "Why do I get the feeling that you're up to something?"

Eagle chuckled, "For such a great warrior, you know so little about women."

Gabe grinned, "I never said I knew *anything* about women!" He sipped at his coffee, as much as having something to do as to have something to hide behind as he sought to discern her intentions.

Gabe rose, tossed the dregs of his coffee aside, looked down at Eagle, "All right. Let's go."

Eagle looked to Ezra, "Black Buffalo is to come too."

"Oh, well alrighty then," declared Ezra as he stood to join the two.

Eagle scratched at the side of the hide lodge, and without waiting for a response, threw open the entry flap and entered. A quick hand motion bid Gabe and Ezra to follow and when they ducked through the entry, they saw not just Chief Sitting Elk, but White Calf's father, the medicine man, Great Owl, and three elders of the tribe. At the chief's motion, Gabe sat beside Black Eagle and Ezra to Gabe's side, all facing the leaders.

The chief motioned to Eagle, who turned sideways to face both Gabe and the leaders, and she explained, "I will interpret for my father. The elders do not understand Spanish or English, so I will interpret for you to understand."

Gabe nodded, and looked to the chief and the elders, "It is an honor to be here. We," he motioned to Ezra and himself, "are grateful to you."

The chief nodded, then began, "We asked you here to tell you we are grateful. In the time you have been with us, you have helped our people in many ways. It is not often that others are helpful to our people, but you have killed to feed our people, and you have fought to save our women." He paused as the others nodded, speaking their agreement and appreciation in soft tones.

Gabe started to respond, but the chief lifted his hand to stop him, and continued. "We were told about Black Buffalo and how he and his mighty war club took the head off a Ute warrior and more. We were also told of you," he nodded toward Gabe, "who moved through the woods like a Spirit Bear and took the lives of many of our enemy with your claws and your arrows." Again, came the mumblings of the elders as they agreed and in their own way showed their appreciation and respect.

The chief turned and picked up a bundle from behind the line of leaders, turned and held before him a headdress, usually worn by medicine men or other chiefs, that was fashioned from the head of a buffalo. The most prominent features were the buffalo horns and the cape from a thick buffalo hide, it was to be worn like a hat, and would resemble the head of a buffalo. The tips of the horns were capped with silver, and the cape was adorned with three feathers on each side that dangled from thin strips of rawhide. The chief handed it to Ezra, "Black Buffalo, you honor us with your courage and commitment to our people."

Ezra hesitated, then reached forward and accepted the gift, holding it as the treasure it was and admiring it as he held it on his crossed legs. "I am greatly honored by this fine gift, chief. I will treasure it and keep it always."

The chief nodded, then turned once again, picked up a small parcel and turned to face the two friends. He looked to Gabe and began, "You have shown you are a friend of the people. Your courage and ways have made our people remember our sacred Spirit Bear. He is white and lives in a faraway land. My father and his father before him knew of this bear who was known as the greatest of all the creatures in the forest. Like you, this bear had hair of gold and white, his claws were long and sharp, and he moved as if he was not there. You are like this bear and you will be known as *Nonoocoo Wox,* White Bear or some will call you Spirit Bear. Some have already said you are as the Claw of the Spirit Bear." He handed Gabe the small parcel, a folded piece of buckskin and as he unfolded it, Sitting Elk said, "That was made by my father's father, and came from the paw of the Spirit Bear. Wear it with honor."

Gabe unfolded the last piece of buckskin to reveal a necklace that held two bear claws with tufts of white hair at their base. The claws were over four inches long and at the base were a creamy white but melded to a glossy black at the tip. The claws rested on a red felt pad, surrounded by colored quills, and hung from a multi-colored coral necklace. It was a magnificent piece of craftsmanship and Gabe lifted his eyes to the chief, "This is beautiful. But this was your father's, I can't take it."

The chief scowled, "It is my honor to give it."

Eagle also scowled at Gabe, gave a slight shake of her head to tell him no, and interpreted for the chief. She leaned toward Gabe and said, "You must take it. If you did not, it would dishonor him. But if you want to give him a gift in return, that would be acceptable."

Gabe nodded, and had come prepared. He knew of the practice of giving and receiving gifts and the custom of the people in such exchanges and he reached inside his tunic and brought out a knife and scabbard. He looked to Eagle and then to the chief, "Then give me the honor of accepting this gift, which was from my father." He handed it to the chief, who reached for it but held his stoic expression. When he held the knife, he was visibly impressed, for it was a Flemish knife, known as the best knives made, with a birch burl handle set behind an engraved nickel silver and brass guard and pommel. The blade was of Damascus steel and had been sharpened to a fine edge. "That knife is from the finest knife makers in Belgium, far across the great waters."

It was a beautifully crafted weapon and the chief marveled at it as he turned it over in his hands, then passed it to the others to examine. He looked to Gabe and Ezra, "You are welcome to be a part of our people. We invite you to become one of the *Hinonoeino.* If you stay with us, you may take a woman as your own and your children will also be *Hinonoeino.*"

Gabe looked from the chief to Eagle, who averted her eyes, but he could see she was smiling, and then to Ezra. The glances they exchanged said they both knew what this meant. He thought to himself, *So, this is what it comes down to, he's thinking of me as a husband for his daughter. Now what am I gonna do?*

12 / Celebration

It was a grand celebration! The feast was sumptuous, the dancing marvelous, and the tale-telling embellished. Never had there been so many great hunters and heroic rescuers at one time in the memory of the elders, who sat alongside one another, grinning and laughing at the antics of the young warriors and rejoicing maidens. They were no different than what Gabe had seen before among the civilized white settlements, when a loved one is lost, and the family gathers for the wake. It often becomes a time of remembrance, laughter, and the sharing of fond memories, many of them a little embossed, in an effort to look to the future instead of the past. The common attempts to erase pain and replace that pain with pleasure, are as age-old as time itself.

Although Gabe and Ezra did not participate in the dance, they did partake of the feast and now sat back, somewhat bloated at their over-indulgence, and watched the others. Ezra's attention was drawn to the sisters, both had paired up with young warriors, and were happy in their dancing. He leaned over to Gabe, "This might be a good time to make our get-away. They look almighty happy," he said, nodding toward the girls.

"So, you're ready to leave 'em, stead o' love 'em?" asked Gabe.

Ezra turned to look at him, "Just 'fore this thing started, Bobcat was talkin' 'bout how she wanted to have two, three babies, just like me! Now, I don' know 'bout you, but that scared the beejeebies outta me!"

Gabe chuckled, "So, the chickens have come home to roost, have they? But, I think I know what you mean. After Sitting Elk talked about takin' a woman and becomin' a part of the tribe, and Black Eagle smilin' at the thought, my feet startin' itchin' somethin' fierce!"

"Maybe we could just get up, casual like, and sneak outta here while they're havin' so much fun," suggested Ezra, looking back at the dancers.

Gabe looked around, located Black Eagle sitting near her father and arrayed in her finery, as were the others. She was a beautiful woman and a woman that would stand beside her man. He had given a lot of thought and prayer to the matter of making her his wife. Yet the banshee of the mountains wailed her invitation every time he seriously considered staying with the Arapaho. The dream and purpose of the men had long been to explore the unknown wilderness and the mountains that beckoned them onward, and to cast that aside was a price more dear than he was willing to pay.

He sucked in a deep breath as he took in the tranquil scene before him, let his eyes linger on Eagle for a moment, until she looked up at him, then he leaned toward Ezra, "Maybe you're right." Ezra nodded and made a casual look around, then stood and retreated from the firelight as if he were answering nature's call and disappeared into the dark.

Gabe made it a point to watch the dancers, smiling and laughing at their moves, and casually looking around the crowd at the many onlookers who occasionally glanced his direction as well. He turned his head slightly, and glanced back at Eagle, saw her looking at him and turned his eyes away. He breathed deep, lifting his shoulders, and slowly stood and walked away.

Ezra had brought their horses to the lodge and was tethering them as Gabe arrived. Without a word, Gabe ducked into the tipi and fetched an armload of gear. Their saddles had been stacked together with the packsaddles and panniers. His first armload was the two saddles of the men. Ezra took his and turned to tend to the bay as Gabe went to Ebony's side, greeted his friend, and lay the blanket on his back. He hefted the saddle in place, reached under his belly for the latigo and soon had his black geared up. They turned to the packhorses and loaded them for their journey and returned to the tipi for their weapons.

Gabe slid the Ferguson into the scabbard on the right side of Ebony, put the pistols in the holsters beside the pommel, and walked around behind the stallion to get his bow. He was surprised to see Black Eagle standing beside the lodge,

Mongol bow and quiver in hand. Sadness showed in her eyes as she slowly lifted the sheathed bow to Gabe.

"You would leave without speaking to Eagle?" she asked quietly.

Gabe stepped closer, took her hands in his and looked into her deep dark eyes, "I didn't think I could stand before you like this, and still leave. You have come to mean a great deal to me."

"And you to me. But I know it is not meant to be that we should be together. You are destined to go far into the wilderness, but my people need me here. I cannot leave them."

"Just as you cannot leave, I cannot stay. There have been those who follow me and bring death on those that I would stay with, I cannot have that happen to you or your people," explained Gabe. Although he hoped the threat of bounty hunters was in the past, there was no way he could be certain of that, and he knew they would always travel with a constant watch on their back trail.

"You will always be welcome if you choose to return," added Eagle, gripping his hands.

The creak of the saddle under Ezra's weight was a rude reminder of the choice already made. Gabe drew Eagle close and the two embraced, moved apart and looked into one another's eyes for one last time. When Eagle released his hands, he stepped back, turned and swung aboard Ebony. He looked down at Eagle, saw tears in her eyes and fought to keep his own in check.

Ezra said, "Tell the sisters goodbye for me, and wish them a happy life!"

"I will. They are young and love comes easily for them," answered Eagle.

They brought heels to the sides of their horses and rode silently from the camp. Believing themselves unseen by the celebrating crowd, they were watched by tear filled eyes as Bobcat waved goodbye from the darkness.

The moon had waned to half, yet the sky was clear, and the diamond speckled black canopied over the two friends as they rode silently in the night. Black Buffalo and Spirit Bear basked in the beauty of the Creator, lifting wondering eyes to the arching milky way that some natives believed to be the cross-over bridge to the hereafter. Gabe's voice cut the silence like a distant bolt of lightning, "It just doesn't seem like there were this many stars in the night-sky back home. I've never seen such a marvel."

They rode due north and Ezra replied, "Well, we both know the error of that statement. But, I am glad that star," pointing to the north star straight before them, "is where it should be. According to what Eagle said, we'll be followin' that one for at least a couple days, 'fore we turn west to the mountains."

Ummhmm, and there I am," chuckled Gabe, pointing to Ursa Major, or the Great Bear constellation. "Too bad there's not a constellation for buffalo!" snickered Gabe, laughing with his friend.

"That's 'cuz we're too busy trompin' on all you Spirit Bears down here!" replied Ezra.

They kept the mountains off their left shoulder and hugged the tree line as much as possible. Riding through the remainder of the night, they came to a brush shrouded creek as the darkness was split by the fine line of grey. They made a comfortable camp on the bank of the chuckling creek and the slow-rising sun painted the mountains with its brush of pink and orange, letting the colors slide down the shoulders of the timber covered crags.

They made a small fire under the wide branches of a rough barked bur oak that stood askew at the edge of the stream, letting what little smoke that came from the long-dried wood sift its way through the thick foliage. Although a little out of the habit of cooking, what with the sisters cooking for them, Ezra took to his task and soon had coffee boiling, strip steaks simmering, and prairie turnips baking. Both men anticipated a good meal before a good day's rest.

"Eagle said the Wind River mountains are about five or six days to the northwest, if we decide to go that way. But she also said there's another mountain range straight north. And that one's about the same distance. The Wind River mountains are in Shoshoni country, while the others, I think she said they were sometimes called the Bighorns, are in Crow country." Gabe was pouring himself a cup of coffee as he talked.

"I thought she said we'd be in Cheyenne country," replied Ezra, checking the steaks.

"We will be, but we'll just pass through it to get to the

mountains. And neither the Crow nor Shoshoni are friendly with the Arapaho."

"So, if we run up against 'em, we just don't talk 'bout the Arapaho, that it?" chuckled Ezra.

"Personally, I'd like to find some way to see all the country and not have to have a run-in with any unfavorable types, of any color. Now, how 'bout we eat and get some sleep?"

13 / Great Basin

The remaining strip steaks and slices of turnip were bunched together in the pan as Ezra stirred them around in the grease from the pork belly. The leftovers from the night before sizzled as he lay the johnnycakes atop the simmering mess. The coffee was boiling in the dancing pot, and he looked up at the trees, anticipating Gabe's return. High overhead, the mid-day sun made its presence felt on Ezra's back as he knelt before the small fire, giving the mixture one last stir before removing the pan to the flat rock beside the smoldering coals.

Gabe came from the trees, brass telescope in hand, showing a broad grin as he greeted his friend, "Smells good, and I'm hungry!"

"Just heated up leftovers, nothing to compare with what the women would be fixin' if they was here with us," replied Ezra, glancing at his friend. "Didja see anything?"

"Absolutely nothing! And I do mean nothing! I ain't never seen so much nothing!" He reached for the coffee pot to pour himself a cup. He lifted his eyes to his friend, "As far as I could see, even with the scope, and lookin' north and north west, this land goes on forever! Just the lookin' at it makes me feel like one o' them red and black ants we keep seein'. I think I saw some pronghorns, but they were gone so fast I'm not sure. Maybe a deer, couple coyotes, and a lot of cactus and sagebrush, but not much else."

"Mountains?" asked Ezra, filling his tin with some of the makins' from the pan.

Gabe followed suit and answered, "Only mountains I could see were these right here behind us."

"But Eagle said these mountains are nothing compared to those further north," implored Ezra, wanting to hear a better answer to his query.

"Ummhmm," replied Gabe, between bites of steak and turnips, "and that just tells me this country is a whole lot bigger than I ever imagined. You know, in all the territory we've covered since we left Pennsylvania, there was an abundance of green, trees, grasses, and more. And rain was a common occurrence, but this country, nothing like it. Behind us, here among the trees, lots of green. But out there," nodding to the north, "little thin lines of green that makes the brown land look like a kids picture puzzle."

"Well, God is a Creator of variety!" pronounced Ezra, wasting little time on his eating.

Gabe picked up a stick, smoothed out the dirt between him and Ezra and began to draw. "Eagle said there were two mountain ranges here," he drew two squiggly lines beside one another on a slant at his left, "and the Wind River comes from between 'em. Now, these other mountains, the Bighorns, are over here." He drew another zig-zag line to his right that came from the top of his dirt map down to the center, "And this same river turns to the north toward these mountains. So, I'm thinkin' we'll head toward the Wind River mountains first, take a look-see, then follow this river to these other mountains. I mean, we're not on a schedule or anything," he declared.

"No, and as far as I know, there's no damsels in distress for you, as the knight in shining armor, to rescue," added Ezra, chuckling.

Gabe chuckled as well, sipped at his coffee, then added, "We're still in friendly Arapaho country, so, how 'bout we travel across some of this country in the daylight and get a better look?"

It was a strange land. New and different from anything they had seen before. With wide vistas and unbroken panoramas, the land seemed to stretch beyond even their imagination. Rolling hills of pale brown, made so by the abundance of buffalo grass waving in the wind, cut with jagged claw marks of runoff ravines and gullies. Where there was any moisture, strips of green divided the plains and mesas, making them stand in contrast to the blue-grey sagebrush and thin Indian grass. Short, broad leafed, blue gramma grass made islands of contrast in the dusty rolling sea. Patches of prickly pear and cholla cactus were interspersed with the sage and rabbit brush.

And the contrast was not limited to plant life. They saw long-eared jackrabbits, grey fox, coyotes, and a herd of about fifty pronghorn antelope. But their biggest surprise was when Gabe called out, "Look yonder!" and pointed to a low plateau to their left.

"Are those horses?" asked Ezra.

"Mustangs! There's gotta be twenty or thirty of 'em. And look at that stallion prancin' around the bunch."

As he spoke, the big paint stallion reared up, pawing at the sky and mane waving in the wind, as he whinnied a challenge to the interlopers in his territory. Even at this distance, the stallion recognized a potential challenger in the big black ridden by Gabe. Ebony let a low rumble come from deep within as if to say, "Anytime, paint, anytime." With one last head shake toward Ebony, the paint stallion pushed his herd off the flat-top and disappeared beyond.

Gabe was pleasantly surprised at the variety and color on the plains. From the hilltop where he scanned the flats with his telescope, he saw an endless land of brown. But now, up close, it held a diversity of plants and colors. The two friends found themselves continually pointing out discoveries to one another. When Ezra first saw the cholla, he called out, "Look! I ain't never seen the same kinda cactus have two different colors of blooms." The yellow and pink blossoms on the stick looking cholla cactus made him stop and marvel. Gabe reined up and turned for a better look.

"And lookee here. There's the flat bladed prickly pear with yellow blooms and right nearby, there's some barrel cactus with bright pink." He pointed to a cactus patch off to their right that held both types that nestled among the rocks. A brown and grey striped lizard stared at them from a hot flat rock amidst the cactus.

Gabe started to turn around in his saddle when the packhorse exploded! He bent in the middle, eyes intent on the ground at his side, all four feet coming off the ground as he jerked the lead rope from Gabe's hand and took off bucking, kicking, snorting, and running. Suddenly he stumbled, went end over end, and lay on his back, kicking and snorting. All the horses were spooked, although nothing like the packhorse, and Gabe had a tight grip on the reins of Ebony and gigged the skittish stallion closer to the downed packhorse. Gabe jumped to the ground, went to the chestnut's head and reached out to try to calm him down. The animal was rocking side to side, obviously in pain, and Gabe saw the right foreleg, bent unnaturally between the knee and fetlock, and knew he had broken a leg. He stroked the gelding's neck, spoke softly to him, and slipped the Bailes pistol from his belt. He eared back the hammer and placed the muzzle behind the horse's ear and pulled the trigger. The blast of the pistol contrasted with the stillness of the prairie and all the horses flinched, as did Gabe and Ezra, but the pack horse lay still, and out of pain.

Gabe stood, went to Ebony, who was trembling as he looked at the packhorse, and stroked his neck and head, speaking softly to him. He looked back to the cactus patch, saw nothing, then to Ezra, "See what caused that?"

"Yup, rattlesnake. He took off into those rocks yonder. And don't ask me to go after him, I don't like snakes!"

"Then, let's get away from here 'fore we lose another'n," responded Gabe.

They quickly stripped the gear and packs from the downed horse and distributed the load among the three horses, and once all was tied down, they started out again. Ezra said, "Now what? One packhorse, especially that little sorrel mare, can't handle this kinda load all the time."

"Then maybe we'll hafta try for one of those mustangs!"

"Ha!" exclaimed Ezra, "That promises to be exciting!"

"Don't it though," replied Gabe, shaking his head at the thought of Ebony confronting that big paint. But they wouldn't have long to wait. It is the nature of a mustang stallion to challenge any and all comers, and to try to take every mare into his harem. And it usually happened in a midnight raid.

14 / Mustangs

"Just how do you propose we go 'bout catchin' one o' them mustangs?" asked Ezra, stoking the fire with some fresh dry wood. They had finished their evening meal and now sat back to reminisce and plan.

"I'm not sure. Never had to try to catch a wild horse before. You got any ideas?" answered Gabe, putting the coffee cup to his lips and looking through the rising vapor to his friend.

Ezra looked at Gabe, "I don't even look like, much less think or act like one o' them vaqueros you've talked about. I do know you're mighty proud of that riata you traded for from the Osage, but it's gonna take more'n pride and book learnin' to catch those horses."

Gabe chuckled, looked into the hot coals of the fire, glassy eyed, then looked at Ezra, "What do the mustangs need most? Water and food! So, if we find where they're getting that, maybe we can figure out a way to trap a couple."

"Well, that's a start. But this is mighty big country and there's probably more'n one place where they can get water," mused Ezra.

"You got a better idea?"

"No, but I'm thinkin'."

Gabe lifted his eyes to the deepening darkness, nodded his head upward and said, "With the moon no more'n a sliver, and the increasing clouds, we won't see enough tonight to get anything done, so, how's about we go to the blankets and tackle the problem in the mornin'?"

"That's the best idea I heard all day!" agreed Ezra as he stood and went to where he had laid his bedroll. "See ya in the mornin'!"

With their constant change from night to day travel, both men tossed about in their blankets before dozing off. The horses had been picketed within reach of both graze and water, and when the men turned in, all three horses stood three legged, heads down and quiet. The men had learned that whenever a horse was tied, tethered, picketed or corralled, it had to be done in such a fashion as to hold them secure, but if the situation demanded, they could eventually work themselves free to find more graze and water and would not die where they stood. Tonight, each of the three horses were picketed, with long lead lines that allowed movement.

The last time Gabe looked at the moon and stars to guess the time, was about an hour past midnight. The cloud cover was lessening but the last sliver of moon hung lazily amidst a handful of stars, seeming to rock the lanterns of the night to sleep. Gabe's eyes finally grew heavy and he rolled to his side, facing the horses and a last glimpse assured him all was quiet.

It was a snort from Ebony that brought Gabe instantly awake. He did not move, but searched the darkness with wide eyes, and saw only the snip of white between flared eyes of Ebony and another snort told Gabe there was danger near. Without moving his body or blankets, he grasped one saddle pistol, and slowly turned to look behind him toward the tree line. There, away from the shadows of the trees and contrasting with the pale colors of the plains, stood the big paint stallion. His bald face glaring in the dim star light and the patch work colors of blood red and white stood in stark contrast to the bland shades of the desert. He looked magnificent, neck arched, mane flashing in the night, muzzle tucked to his chest, one hoof pawing the darkness before him and he seemed to dance to the rhythm of the cicadas. He was a part of the night and the nocturnal creatures were not silenced by his presence. A night hawk circled and cried his encouragement and a great owl questioned the disturbance to his nap. Far away a lonesome coyote paged his lover, but his cry went unanswered.

Gabe turned back to look at Ebony and even in the darkness, the glistening midnight coat shone, and the thick mane danced as the big stallion side stepped, tugging at his tether. Gabe looked from the paint to his black and rose from his blankets to go to his friend, hoping to settle him down. But the stallion paid little mind to his friend, hearing instead the cry of the ancients, the challenge that brought forth more than either could understand, but the black was determined to answer. Gabe reached up and slipped the halter from his friend's head and stood aside as the stallion reared up and whinnied his answer to the challenge of the paint. Ebony lunged forward, head extended, teeth bared and eyes blazing as he charged toward the challenger.

There is something primitive that beats in the heart of the male of each species, a drive that rises to a challenge or a dare. That is why fathers allow and sometimes encourage their progeny to stand before any challenge, the meeting of those contests are oftentimes the building blocks of manhood. It is not the winning, nor the losing, but the willingness to meet whatever threatens, and to stand for what he holds sacred or dear. While a mother's reaction is to protect by sheltering, a father's is to protect by meeting that challenge and sending it on its way, if possible. But the failure to stand often has greater and costlier consequences than the losing of the conflict. And man does not stop to reason out his actions, he simply responds.

Gabe stood, halter in hand, and fear in his heart, as he watched Ebony kick clods of dirt in his haste to meet the paint. Ezra had risen and came to Gabe's side, rifle in hand, and asked, "Why'd you let him go?"

Gabe nodded toward the paint and both men watched as the two stallions met. Both reared up, pawing at the other, teeth bared and craning their necks around to try to inflict wounds. They dropped to all fours, biting and circling, using their heads as battering rams, moving faster than either of the men had seen before.

Behind them Ezra's bay and the little sorrel mare had turned to watch the battle and beyond the fight shadows moved about and the men knew those were the other horses in the paint's herd. Screams and whinnies came from the combatants, the soil was turned up and showed black in the night, as a big glistening shadow circled the flashes of white and blood red. The paint whirled around and kicked at Ebony, but the black was too quick, and the hind hooves of the paint caught nothing but air, making him stumble, but he quickly caught himself and turned to face the black. Ebony feinted with his teeth at the paint's shoulder, but when the herd stallion used his head to try to knock Ebony aside, the black ducked under and sunk his teeth into the side of the paint, eliciting a scream and stagger to the side as he fought to get away.

Ebony stepped back, sidestepping and tossing his head, his mane flying, and lunged forward, putting his head to the side, he used his chest to ram the paint, knocking him to the ground. Ebony reared up, pawing the sky and brought his hooves stabbing down on the neck and head of the paint. He battered the downed stallion again and again, then stepped back, allowing the paint to get to his feet.

Even in the dim light of the night, patches of blood could be seen on the white splotches of the stallion, who staggered back away from Ebony. Ebony stretched out his hoof, pawing at the air, as he tucked his muzzle to his chest, arching his neck, and snorting. He pranced forward, pawing the air with one hoof, then the other, and as he moved, the paint retreated. Suddenly the black reared up, letting out a screaming whinny as he pawed the air, challenging the paint. But the herd stallion knew he had met his better and with head hanging, he stumbled away. He stayed near the tree line, ignoring the herd that waited beyond.

Ebony pranced around a little, then walked to Gabe. He stretched out his muzzle and Gabe spoke softly, reassuringly, and stroked the black's head and neck. He lifted the halter to put it on his stallion, but the big horse stepped back, bobbing his head, then quickly turned and took off at a run toward the herd.

Gabe stood still, watching, but the darkness kept him from seeing what was happening, and the shadows moved toward Ebony. Then he heard nickering, and an occasional squeal, but nothing more. Ezra asked, "You think he'll come back?"

"I hope so, but, if he don't . . ." and he left the thought hang in the darkness. The comment was as much a question and an expression of doubt and fear. Gabe had never thought he could lose the big black, they had been the best of friends since they first met, but this was the place of the wild animals and just as it brought out the wild in Ebony, it had also tugged at the primitive in both men.

"Guess we'll just have to wait and see. Can't do much in the dark," surmised Gabe, turning back to the smoldering coals and the warm coffee pot. He knew he wouldn't sleep the rest of the night and there was no sense in trying. But that didn't mean they couldn't have some coffee and maybe something more. Ezra walked back to the other horses, talked to them and checked their tethers, then returned to the fire to join his friend.

15 / Resolved

The warm muzzle nibbled at Gabe, bringing him instantly awake to see the face of Ebony, nuzzling him, nibbling at his ears. Gabe reached up to stroke the face of the big black, and swore the stallion was smiling at him. With a quick look around in the dim light of early morning, he pushed his blankets aside and stood beside his friend. He spoke softly to wake Ezra and continued to stroke Ebony's neck and talk to him.

"Where's all your girlfriends, boy? They run off?" Although he knew the big horse didn't understand the words, he knew he understood the mood and manner, and Gabe continued to show his love for his faithful friend. As Ezra came from his blankets, Gabe said, "I think Ebony's up to something. I'm gonna go with him." He had grabbed a long lead line and fashioned a slip-knot halter and slipped it over his head and draped the lead over his neck. He bent to pick up the saddle but was pushed away by Ebony's head. He turned and said, "What was that for?" and scratched the forehead of the black, attention the horse always enjoyed. He reached again for the saddle and received another push from Ebony. He looked to Ezra, "I guess I'm goin' bareback. Hurry up and come along." He grabbed a handful of mane and swung aboard the tall stallion, looked back at Ezra as he did the same on his bay.

Ebony eagerly stepped out and took to a thin game trail that followed the creek beside the camp. They pushed through thick brush and tall grasses going deeper into the mountains. Ebony turned to follow a small feeder stream that took a steep climb up a narrow draw. Gabe heard the unseen chuckling stream as it cascaded over the rocks rushing to the valley below. His first glimpse showed the stream was no more than a long stride across, but it hurried on its way. The trail cut back on itself several times but stayed in the trees, a blend of juniper and ponderosa that stretched long limbs of clustered needles high above.

Even though it was a steep climb, Gabe knew they had gone about a mile up the narrow canyon when he heard the splashing and crashing of a waterfall. With only a glimpse through the trees, he guessed the little creek fell close to a hundred feet to the pool below and the morning sun painted wispy rainbows in the mist. Another switchback and the trail opened to a brilliant green hanging valley. Surrounded by rocky crags, the beautiful basin held about thirty or forty acres of tall grass with scattered clusters of pine and fir trees that framed the tranquil scene. Several heads of the horse herd came up to see the new arrivals and Gabe knew they had found the safe haven of the mustangs.

This was a bigger herd than what they had seen below with the paint stallion. Although some of the horses looked familiar, most were not, and several had colts by their side. Gabe and Ezra sat quietly, watching the animals graze. Several of the colts and yearlings ran and kicked and bucked on spindly legs as they cavorted about, enjoying the rising sun that painted the bottoms of what few clouds hung in the quickly bluing sky. The few mares that had stared at the newcomers, now casually lowered their heads into the deep grass, taking their morning graze. Gabe laid the lead rope on Ebony's neck and leaned forward, one hand on the stallion's withers, and watched. Ebony started a slow walk toward the herd, and Ezra and his bay hung back. Gabe had slipped his riata over one shoulder and his head when they left the camp, and touched it for reassurance now, letting Ebony have his head and trusting his friend completely.

The big black stopped about thirty yards from the herd, lifted his head high and nickered. Several of the mares quickly lifted their heads and looked at the stallion and two began to walk slowly toward him. Gabe saw they were mares, but without a colt at their side, and guessed them to be about two going on three years old. The one in the lead was a confident stepping grulla, dark legs and mane, big bright eyes, and she tossed her head and gave an answering nicker. She came close, her attention focused on the black, but obviously seeing Gabe sitting astride. She stopped about ten feet away, looked at the stallion, then at Gabe and back at the stallion who stood quiet and waiting. One tentative step, then another, and another and she was soon nuzzling the big stallion and they crooked necks together, but the mare kept a vigilant eye on the man.

The second mare watched the interplay with the grulla and the black. She was a steel dust grey with black mane and tail, one white stocking at the front and a diamond blaze on her forehead. She stood watching, head high, occasionally bobbing, but never taking her eyes off the black. While Ebony was sixteen hands, the two mares were just under fifteen hands, but both were well built with good chests and rumps, strong necks and soft eyes. Gabe was impressed with Ebony's choice in mares and believed if he had his pick of the herd, he would probably pick the same two. But what to do now was the question.

Without turning around, and without raising his voice, he asked Ezra, "Can you come up here, a little closer?" His answer came as he heard the bay pushing through the tall grass and coming near. "Did you bring an extra lead line or anything?"

"Ummhmmm," answered Ezra.

"Can you make a loop at the end; one you can drop over the head of one of these mares?"

"Maybe, but then what? I don't think they'll like it much, and we don't have a saddle horn to hold 'em."

"I dunno, but they're curious, just let 'em come near and do their sniffin' and such. If it looks possible, then do whatever you think will work. I don't know anymore about this than you," declared Gabe. "But, whatever we do, we'll need to try to do it together, cuz if one spooks, they both will."

The men sat, watching and unmoving, occasionally speaking softly just so the horses would be used to their voices. The dirty pale brown grulla came alongside Ebony, watching the man carefully and sniffing at his leg, stepped back and leaned closer for another sniff. She nibbled at his pantleg with her lips, always looking up at Gabe, watching for anything. She started to bite, but Gabe jerked his leg back and the grulla jumped away, eyes wide showing white, and stood well out of reach. She tossed her head and looked away, took a couple steps away, then craned her neck around for another look.

The steeldust was more interested in the bay than the man atop him. The bay was a gelding but was still interesting to the grey mare and she reached out with her nose to sniff his muzzle, then twisted down to nibble at his neck, but the bay stepped back out of her reach. She stood, looking at the gelding, then apparently became curious in the man and came to the side of the horse to look closer at the man. Her actions were much the same as the grulla and Ezra was just as busy watching the grey as Gabe was at watching the grulla.

"Have you made your loop yet?" asked Gabe, keeping his eyes on the mare.

"Doin' it now," answered Ezra, moving slowly as he tried to not alarm the grey.

"I'm holding mine down by my leg, and if she comes near,

I'm gonna try to ease it over her head. Not gonna pull it tight, if I can help it, but we'll see," explained Gabe.

"Will do," answered Ezra and lowered the loop beside his leg.

Within moments, the grey moved alongside the bay and pushed against Ezra's leg. With his free hand, Ezra slowly reached down near the muzzle of the grey and let her get a smell. He slowly came back erect and sat, watching the mare shoulder the bay and move away, then come back close. As she neared, Ezra slowly moved the lead rope's loop and slipped it over the mare's head, almost unnoticed, but the touch of the rope to her neck spooked her and she jerked back, but just a couple steps. Ezra let the rope go slack, and the mare tossed her head, but didn't move away.

Gabe's attention was focused on the grulla, *that is a mighty pretty horse,* he thought as he watched it come near. Even with the tangled mane, burrs in its tail, and the rough coat, she was an exceptional animal. She nuzzled next to Ebony, rubbing her face on his neck and stepped back, then close again. Gabe slipped the riata over her head, left it slack, but she acted as if she didn't notice. Then she moved a few steps away, and felt the tension, and spooked. She reared up, tossed her head and pawed at the sky, snorted and as her feet hit the ground she lunged ahead, kicking dirt clods with her hind hooves as she leaned into her lunge. Gabe grabbed at the rope with both hands, caught a handful of mane with one, and dug heels to Ebony to follow the mare. Within two long strides the mare had hit the end of the rope and jerked

Gabe down along Ebony's neck, but the stallion matched her speed and within moments the two horses were racing nose to tail across the basin.

The sudden movement of the big black and the grulla startled both the steeldust and the bay, and both took after the fleeing pair, the lead rope on the grey drawing taut. Ezra wrapped the end of the rope around his left wrist, held tight to mane and rope with his right hand, and leaned into the race, legs clamping on the sides of the bay as if glued. The herd split, some running ahead, others to the side, some just stepping out of the way, but every eye was on the race.

Ebony was quickly beside the grulla, and bumped her shoulder with his, slamming the two bodies together with Gabe's leg between. The grulla stumbled, but kept running and Ebony leaned toward her, pushing her into the taller grass. She started to slow and dropped to a canter, then a trot and with Ebony still leaning beside her, she slowed to a walk. Gabe slowly coiled the loose riata, watching the mare as she stood, sides heaving and head down. She tried to sidestep, but the ground was boggy from the spring water that fed the little creek. With one foot deep in the mud, she stopped and stood, breathing heavily, but unmoving. Gabe reached down to touch her neck, speaking softly as he did and she flinched at his touch, but did not move away. He continued speaking, and slowly moved his hand along the side of her neck, then to her withers and her back and to her neck again.

Ezra's bay had kept pace with the grey and both horses had followed the lead of Gabe's black and the grulla. When the two leaders came to a stop at the edge of the bog, the steeldust kept going and found herself, spread legged, all four hooves in the bog and unable to move. Ezra still had the lead rope around his wrist and was leaning to the side off the bay and decided he would have better control on the ground. He slipped off the bay and stood between the two, the steeldust staring at him wide-eyed with nostrils flaring. Ezra spoke to the grey, holding out one hand toward her nose and slowly stepped closer, but the grey emitted a snot filled snort that splattered all over his hand and arm and chest. Ezra made a face, fought the urge to step back and wipe it off, and stepped closer, letting the mare get another sniff. *This ain't gonna be easy,* he thought, shaking his head.

16 / Contest

His silent thought, read by the grey, was like a challenge to the mustang. She reared back on her haunches, her front hooves making sucking sounds as she pulled them from the bog. Rearing up and shaking her head, she fought against the restraining rope held by Ezra. At her first move, Ezra dug in his heels, pulled the rope over his thigh, his right hand holding it taut below his hip, his left gripping tightly to the extended rope as he watched the muddy grey rear high. As she tossed her head side to side, Ezra answered with a jerk that brought her down to all fours and she fought both the man and the muck. Leaning back on her haunches, throwing her head side to side, she struggled for air, but the ever-tightening rope rationed it as she fought. Ezra continued to speak softly as he slid his hands along the rope, moving closer to the grey who now stood spread legged and staring.

Gabe had given the grulla a little slack and looked over at Ezra, now more than ankle deep in the bog and slowly approaching the grey. That moment of inattention was all the grulla needed and she lunged to the side, pulling the rope taut in Gabe's hands, and with another leap the grulla was off and running, dragging Gabe behind. He splattered mud as he landed on his face, struggling to get his feet under him, but was jerked into the bog, cattails, and grass that cushioned his fall, but made the dragging easy for the grulla. Gabe bounced through the grass, the tall stalks whipping at his face and hands, but he had wrapped the riata around his left wrist and held tightly with his right. Suddenly the grulla stopped, turning to look at her anchor, and Gabe quickly turned around, still sitting, but with his feet toward the horse. She was staring at him, sides heaving, head down and giving him a stare that dared him to come closer. Gabe returned the glare and slowly came to his feet, allowing no slack in the riata, and spoke softly to the horse. "Now look, girl, we're gonna be friends so you might as well get used to the idea," he began, moving ever closer to the grulla.

Ezra saw Gabe do his trailblazer act, shook his head as he laughed, but kept his eye on the grey. Behind her were a few scattered ponderosa, standing tall and reminding Ezra of armored centurions guarding a palace, and he had an idea. He gave a little slack in the rope, and began walking closer, each step a sucking sound as he pulled his feet from the muck. He was thankful for his high-topped moccasins, held secure by the wrap around his calf, but he knew he would have to give them a good soaking if they were to be used again. As he neared the grey, she fought for footing, moving back from the approaching man. Wary of him, she side-stepped, and was soon free of the bog. She stood trembling, watching Ezra, and backed away from him, drawing nearer the tall pines.

Ezra moved slow, one cautious step, wait, another, wait, and the pair of untrusting companions of the hanging valley, were soon near the ponderosa. Ezra stepped beside the tree, held the rope tight with his right hand and whipped the end around the trunk with his left. The grey spooked and jerked back, but not before Ezra had the rope around the trunk and anchored fast. He tied the rope off, stepped back and stood watching and talking to the grey, trying to settle her down and move her closer to the tree to give slack to the rope and loosen it around her neck. One step was all that was necessary, and she lifted her head, sucking in deep gulps of air, and looking sidelong at Ezra. He stood still, speaking lowly, and watching as the mare relaxed.

Gabe sneaked a look at Ezra and grinned when he saw the grey tied off at the tree. With another quick look at the grulla, he searched for a tree, near enough and big enough to tether the mare. Another ponderosa beckoned, although not as big as he hoped, he thought it would be ample and began to calculate his moves to maneuver the grulla near the tree. But she seemed to read his mind, as the female species often does, and jerked her head to the side, spun on her heels and took off through the tall grass, Gabe sliding on his rump, legs extended before him to part the way.

The grulla's human anchor bouncing behind her, the

mare had her head high, mane and tail flying, as she flew by some of the herd that Gabe was certain were cheering her on as they bobbed their heads and some even letting out a nicker. But once again, the heavy anchor took its toll and the grulla came to a stop and turned to face the mudball behind her. Gabe sat a moment, wiping the mud from his face and eyes, glaring at the grulla who bobbed her head and showed her teeth which Gabe interpreted as a horselaugh. He shook his head, "Yeah, you laugh now, but I'm gonna have the last laugh, even if it kills me! You ain't winnin' this contest!"

The grulla had unknowingly brought them to just the right place as she stood close by a big spruce that towered over the nearby trees. Gabe slowly stood, stomped his feet to rid them of some muck, and began moving closer to the grulla and the spruce, coiling the riata as he approached. He moved to the side, dropping his eyes to the ground and watching the mare out of the corner of his eyes as he worked closer to the tall spruce. He moved slowly, talking low, keeping the coil at his left side, hip high, ready to drop it over his thigh and make a stand if necessary, but the grulla stood still, watching. He walked behind the tree and around the far side, and with a quick flick of the rope, had the grulla tethered tight. He tied it off, stood and wiped mud from his hands and front, looking at the mare, "Now I've gotchu!"

Gabe walked away from the trees, whistled for Ebony and watched the big black come trotting up, head high, and prancing. Gabe shook his head, "What're you so happy about?" and reached out to stroke the stallions head. He looked around for Ezra, saw him coming toward him astride his bay, and waited.

"I see you finally decided to quit playin' in the mud!" declared Ezra, laughing.

"You don't look much better!" answered Gabe, nodding at the mud that covered the lower half of his friend. Both men laughed as Ezra slid to the ground and looked back at the two mares, now standing and watching the big stallion and his friends.

"Now what?" asked Ezra.

"Well, it's either we move our camp up here, or we take the mares down to our camp. I think it'd be easier to move the camp up here, but I don't wanna leave them tied up and us take off and they get choked off or somethin'," answered Gabe.

Ezra chuckled, "I noticed a bit of a pool over there just inside the trees, looked big enough to take a bath in, so . . ."

By mid-day they had moved their camp into the hanging valley, near the spring at the upper end and well under the tall ponderosa. They began building a brush corral for the horses, making it large enough for all their horses and to include some graze and water. Using interlaced branches, standing trees, and some of the lead ropes, the corral was finished by late afternoon and they stood looking at one another as Ezra asked, "How we gonna do this?"

"I figger to use Ebony, snub the mares up close, and bring 'em along, one at a time, and put 'em in," replied Gabe.

"I don't think it'll be as easy as you make it sound," answered Ezra, "but we need to get with it so we can be done 'fore dark."

Gabe sidled the black up next to the grey, dropped his riata loop over her head as she struggled against the tree-tethered rope. He snubbed her close to Ebony's side, waited for Ezra to undo the rope from the tree and get aboard his bay. When seated, he came close on the other side and snubbed her near, keeping the lead rope tight. Then they walked the mare between them and into the brush corral, Ezra jumping down at the make-shift gate and Gabe taking her within the enclosure. He reached down and slipped his riata and the rope from her neck just as she jumped sideways and spun to charge at the gate, but Ezra had pushed it closed and stymied, she spun around and paced the perimeter. Gabe coiled the rope and riata and rode to the gate, the two timing his escape when the mare was on the far side.

They repeated their maneuver with the grey and put the sorrel mare packhorse and the bay and Ebony in the corral with the mares and secured the gate. The men walked the outside perimeter, checking for any weak spots in the brush, patching it as necessary and soon stood together, looking over the gate at the horses. They were getting acquainted with one another with sniffing, an occasional bite, a random kick, all to determine the hierarchy of the herd. The men turned away and went to the stack of gear and began laying out their camp. They knew they would be here at least a couple days, if not more, and they determined to make it as comfortable as possible.

For two days, the men worked with the mares, snubbing them up to their horses, walking them around the valley, talking all the while. Late the first day, they strapped on blankets, snubbed them up again and worked their way with another circuit of the valley. The second day was more of a challenge as they tried to put the packsaddles on the mares. It took considerable effort, Gabe aboard Ebony, snubbing the mare alongside, while Ezra put on the blankets and packsaddles. But by the end of the day, the mares were responding well, and they thought they were ready to resume their journey.

"Even though they're doin' better, I think it'd be best if we get a little experience on the trail 'fore we put load on 'em. We can make it by loadin' up our horses and the sorrel like we done before," suggested Ezra.

"You're prob'ly right. Wouldn't want 'em to get spooked and run off with all our supplies," remarked Gabe.

They were sitting by the smoldering coals, enjoying the night sky and their coffee as they listened to the night sounds of nighthawks, coyotes, an occasional owl, when the snort and snarl of a mountain lion brought them to their feet.

"What was that?" asked Ezra.

"How should I know?" answered Gabe.

"But, you got educated at the university, you're supposed to know ever'thing!"

"They don't teach that stuff in the university you know."

The sudden spit and cry of the big cat froze the men as they stood beside the fire. Gabe reached for his rifle, checked the load and took a couple steps toward the trees. Ezra picked up his rifle, checked the loads and followed his friend. He spoke in a whisper from behind him as he asked, "You sure you wanna do this? Go out after him, I mean."

"I ain't goin' nowhere. But I reckon we better keep watch through the night. You go ahead and turn in. I'll walk the camp."

17 / Cougar

The caterwauling wail pierced the darkness and riddled the shadows with fear. The spits and snorts that followed added to the fright and made the horses in the brush corral huddle together and move about as one. Gabe had been leaning against a tall spruce, doing his best to avoid the patches and drips of resin, but when the cat made himself known, he stepped away from the tree, searching the woods and the grassland for any movement. The moon was just waxing from the first quarter, but the stars shone bright in the cloudless sky. Gabe's night vision allowed him to see into the meadow, and gave limited sight into the trees, but this creature of the night would only be seen when he allowed his prey to know that death stalked the shadows.

Gabe knew the cry came from the upper end of the valley and closer to the rocky crags that bordered the basin, but the silence that followed betrayed nothing of his movements. Suddenly a screaming cry came from the far side and Gabe felt a twinge of relief, thinking the cat was moving away. But an answering cry came from the trees at the upper end and Gabe gripped his rifle tighter, hugging it close to his chest. His eyes moved rapidly from one tree to another, then across the meadow and to the far tree line. He saw the shadows of the horse herd milling about, obviously nervous at the presence of the predator as colts huddled with their mothers.

He stepped back into the trees, turned and walked by the brush corral. He spoke as he moved, letting the horses know he was near, and walked around the perimeter of the corral, checking for any weaknesses, but seeing none, he returned to his chosen place beside the big ponderosa. He dropped to one knee, set the Ferguson at his side, butt on the ground and scanned the clearing. The horses had moved to the lower end but were still jittery and moving about. A big roan mare had assumed the leadership of the herd and pushed them along the north edge, moving them closer to their camp.

The night grew quiet, the only sounds coming from the occasional yip of a coyote or cry of the nighthawk. An insomniac squirrel chattered above Gabe, scolding him for the loss of sleep, but Gabe paid little attention. He was focused on the movement of the herd, counting on them warning him of the cougar's presence. Suddenly a scream from the brush corral jolted Gabe and he spun and took off toward the horses at a run, earing back the hammer on the Ferguson as he moved. He brought the rifle to his shoulder as he neared the corral but the screams, whinnies, and ruckus among the horses stifled his move. He searched for the cougar, wanting a shot, but the dust whirled, the thin shaft of light from the sliver of the moon doing little to illumine the corral, and the horses running, rearing, kicking and screaming filled him with dread.

He heard the impact of hooves hitting something, not seeing if it was the cougar or another horse. Then the glistening black coat of Ebony shone as he reared high, eyes showing white, as he came down, stabbing his hooves into the dust cloud below. Again, he reared, head cocked to the side, mane whipping in the air, and again he stabbed down. The other horses had huddled on the far side, prancing and pushing against the brush barrier. Gabe saw the low form of the big cat, tail swishing back and forth, teeth bared as he snarled at the big black who reared high above. With a quick aim through the brush, Gabe fired the Ferguson and the resulting roar and stab of flame briefly illuminated the corral, but the impact of the bullet blossomed red, knocking the cougar to the side just as the hooves of the angry stallion came down with all the force and weight of the majestic Andalusian. Again and again, he stabbed and bit until his anger abated and his energy waned. Then with a toss of his head, he trotted to the other horses, put his butt to them and faced the carcass of the cougar as the champion protector he was.

Gabe had hurriedly reloaded and now stood at the gate, looking toward the horses, as Ezra's voice split the darkness, "Looks like you got him."

"But . . ." started Gabe, when a screeching cry came from deep in the trees that told of the second cougar's approach. It was not the practice of nocturnal predators to let their presence be known, but this animal sensed the loss of his companion and let loose a threatening cry of stalking vengeance. Ezra had his rifle in hand, and Gabe brought his to full cock. He motioned to his friend that he would circle the corral, and Ezra was to remove the carcass and check on the horses. Gabe spoke to the horses, then slowly started his circuitous trek. He wanted to be between the cougar and the horses, and hopefully prevent another attack. He did not know if any of the animals had been injured, but that would come later, now he had a job to do.

He moved slowly, not wanting to make himself a target, but wanting to protect the horses and find the cougar before he attacked. Gabe searched the trees, unable to pierce the dark shadows, but watching for movement. Even in the darkness with nothing but black and shadows, movement could catch a miniscule shaft of light and betray its presence. He kept the brush barrier to his left side, moving carefully, sometimes sidestepping to keep his eyes on the woods. The horses seemed to be settling down since Ezra removed the carcass of the first cougar and stayed inside the barrier, talking and touching, reassuring. He held his rifle at the ready but spoke to the horses quietly.

All he heard was a slight creak from a branch of the big ponderosa, but Gabe ducked down, tucking his head in his shoulders as he hunched, but the long streak of tan fur hit him with enough force to knock him to his face, causing him to fire the rifle into the air. He felt stabbing pain in his shoulders as he jumped to his feet, but the bared teeth of the cougar were before his face and he pushed out with both arms to knock the cougar to the side as both fell to the ground.

They were face to face in the dirt, his rifle already discharged and out of reach, was useless and he twisted to the side, knowing the cougar would use his back legs and claws to try to disembowel him. The long claws tore at his buckskins and he felt his skin tear. He had a forearm against the neck of the lion, and he snatched his pistol from his belt, cocking it as he drew. He fought to bring the muzzle away from his chest and jerked the trigger as he did. The big lead ball tore a gouge along the cougar's chest, pierced its throat, barely missing Gabe's arm, and exploded out the back of the cat's neck. But the lion still fought, and Gabe pushed against its now bloody neck, grabbing at his knife behind his shoulders, brought it to bear and stabbed at the chest of the cougar, fighting for every move and breath. The short stabbing strokes drove the knife deep into the cougar's chest, again and again, as the cougar clawed at his hip and tried to bite his face. Gabe smelled death every time the cougar growled or screamed, and he fought to keep his teeth away. He plunged the knife into the side of the beast, then twisted the blade and dug deep into the gut of the animal, forcing death on the big cat.

Finally, the monstrous feline fell limp, and Gabe fought free of the death grip of the long claws, staggered to his feet, bloody from shoulders to his feet, buckskins hanging in strips. He breathed deep, fell against the stacked brush of the corral and slid to his side, rolled to his face and let the blackness envelop him.

Ezra shook him, "Gabe, Gabe!" But his friend neither moved nor spoke. His breathing was shallow, and he was covered with blood. Ezra scooped him up and took him to his blankets, stretched him out and began to examine his friend. He shook his head as he went to the packs to get everything he needed. When he returned, he tore a linsey Woolsey shirt in strips, soaked some in water from the coffee pot, and began to cleanse the many wounds. Gabe's right hip was shredded and bleeding. Ezra reached into the parfleche for the sinew and needle and began to stitch the long deep cuts. As he finished up, the flow had been stanched, and he wiped the hip clean. There were bite marks, punctures, and deep clawed cuts at his shoulder and upper arm. Ezra threaded some more sinew and continued his patch work stitching.

They had gathered some poplar inner bark and some red buds from the aspen when they first came to the mountains before meeting the Arapaho, and he lay it on the flat rock by the fire and began making poultices. He placed the poultices on each of the wounds, bound them with thin strips of buckskin made from Gabe's shredded britches. He sat back on his heels, looked the patient over and satisfied with his work, he pulled the blanket up. Now it was wait and see.

18 / Recovery

Ezra busied himself gathering plants he knew could be used to tend to Gabe. He found a patch of glacier Lily with its big yellow blooms and clipped several leaves. He added some goldenrod and plantain, then after checking on his patient, he took his bay for a quick ride to the flats and gathered some sage and willow sprouts. Their supply of poplar bark, leaves and buds was soon gone, and he began making poultices with the goldenrod, plantain, and sage. He hung the lily leaves to dry to make a tea, but that would have to wait a day or two.

Gabe stirred, mumbled and pushed off the blankets. Ezra stuffed a blanket under his head and convinced him to chew on the willow sprouts. "Now, hold still so I can get your poultices changed." Gabe didn't respond but lay his head back to chew on the sprigs and let Ezra do his work. He cleaned the wounds, applied the poultices, had to take an additional stitch in his hip, then bound everything with soft buckskin.

He fixed a stew with the last of the venison, choosing to

use up the fresh meat and reserve the smoked meat. When he tried to get Gabe to eat some, he was unable to rouse him. He felt his head, his hand coming away wet with sweat, and knew he had a fever. He brewed a tea with the remaining willow sprigs and poured as much into his mouth as he would take. The cold cloth, soaked in fresh spring water, was applied to his forehead, neck and armpits and within a couple hours, the fever had dropped, and Gabe fell asleep and it appeared to be deep and restful.

By morning, the fever was back, and Gabe tossed and turned, mumbling incoherently, sweating and kicking off his blankets. Ezra brewed some tea from the lily leaves and held Gabe erect enough to make him take a good amount, then encouraged him to chew on the willow sprouts. Ezra checked the bandages, changing as many as necessary and began making more poultices. It was a long day of tending to the struggling Gabe, but by late afternoon he seemed to be resting better. Ezra knew he needed some fresh meat and decided to try for some deer he had seen near the spring.

By the morning of the second day after the confrontation with the mountain lions, Gabe stirred awake and looked around, tried to sit up and felt pain in most every part of his body. Ezra was hunched over the fire, tending to something in a pot when he heard the weak question of his friend, "What's a man gotta do to get some coffee?"

Ezra turned, saw Gabe trying to sit up and went to his side to give him some help. He answered, "There's other things you need more'n coffee."

He twisted around to look at Ezra, saw concern written on his face and asked, "Did you get the cat?"

"No, you did. But he did a number on you 'fore he croaked."

"Is there any place on my body he didn't shred?" asked Gabe, wincing at the pain of moving.

"I think your belly, an' your left leg's alright, but the rest of you, well, let's just say it resembled a fresh batch of pemmican more'n it should."

Ezra fetched him a cup of coffee, folded a blanket to put behind him so he could sit up more comfortably, and returned to the fire to pour him a bowl of stew. Made with fresh venison and simmered for hours, the broth laden stew was exactly what Gabe needed to restore his strength. Although the stew was nourishing, and he felt much better after consuming two bowls, he looked at Ezra as he asked, "How long you think it'll take 'fore I can be up an' about?"

"That's up to you, maybe a day or two, but I'm thinkin' you'll find it a little difficult to sit a saddle with those claw marks on your rump!"

Gabe winced, moved a little trying to get comfortable, and said, "He got me there too, huh?"

"Just one side, same side as most of the rest of it, but it's startin' to heal purty good."

"So, if I kinda sit sidesaddle, maybe we can give it a try?"

"No need to be in a hurry. I saw a huntin' party, maybe ten or twelve Cheyenne, maybe."

Gabe scowled, "When?"

"This mornin' early. Looked like they come from the far side o' these mountains and were headin' north across the flats."

"Packin' anything?"

"Yeah, looked like a couple elk, and maybe a buffalo, some deer. Figgered they was done with the hunt an' headed home."

"Then, if we go back to travelin' at night, and go northwest, should be alright, you think?"

"Prob'ly. If you think you can handle it."

"You been workin' with the new horses any?"

"As much as I could. I think they'll be alright after we are on the trail a night or two."

"Good. Then I'll try to move around some today, and maybe by dusk, we can move out," surmised Gabe, looking to his friend for confirmation.

Ezra grinned, nodded, and returned to the fire for a bowl of his own stew.

Ezra had fashioned Gabe a crutch from an aspen sapling and the patient hopped around the camp, trying to make himself useful and failing. Ezra worked with the new horses, familiarizing them with the halters and packsaddles and in general, being handled by men. As the sun lay cradled in a notch in the western mountains, Ezra looked at his friend, "Whatchu think? You wanna try it or you need another day?"

"No, let's give it a try. If we don't make it very far, at least we'll be away from here."

The moon gave little light, waxing from new moon phase, but the night was clear, and the stars were bright as the men started from the hanging valley to make their way to the flats and start toward the south end of the Wind River mountains. It took Gabe a few tries before he found a reasonably comfortable position atop his saddle, but Ebony's smooth gait made it easy on him, even as they descended the switchback trail that followed the creek to the valley below. When they broke from the trees, Gabe twisted around trying to find a more comfortable position and a quick glance to the trees made him do a double take. He spoke softly to Ezra, "Did you see that?"

"See what?" asked his friend, at the front of the group and holding to the lead of the two mustangs. Gabe led the loaded sorrel packhorse and pulled her alongside as they kept to the trail.

Gabe answered, "I could swear I saw a pair of orange eyes looking at us from the trees."

Ezra reined up and let Gabe draw up beside him, "Where?"

Gabe twisted in his saddle, pointed to the edge of the thick juniper, "There."

They watched for a moment, then Ezra said, "Whatever it was, maybe it's gone. Let's keep going."

But Gabe wasn't satisfied and continued to watch their backtrail. Although the terrain had changed from timber covered hills and mountains to rolling flat lands scarred by ravines, gullies, and scattered sagebrush and cacti, the starlight did little to ease his concern and curiosity. He made another twist in his saddle and lifted his eyes to the far side of the ravine they followed, and a long shadow moved, and orange eyes flickered for just an instant. Gabe caught his breath and unconsciously leaned toward the sight, and saw another shadowy form, and another. He gigged his horse to move beside Ezra, "Uh, we've got a problem."

Ezra looked sideways at him, "Orange eyes again?"

"Wolves, at least three of 'em. They're followin' along on the other bank of this ravine."

"I thought Whiskey was a little skittish, musta smelled 'em."

"Whiskey?"

"Yeah, that's the name of my horse, didn't you know that?"

"Since when?"

"Just now. Been thinkin' on it though. Your's is Ebony cuz he's black, an' this'uns dark brown an' black, same as whiskey, so, why not?"

"You're a preacher's son, that's why not! What'd your father say?"

"Uh, I think we need to be thinkin' about a more pressing problem!" he nodded his head toward the shadowy forms across the ravine. Outlined against the brown bunch grass of the flats, four stealthy shadows moved silently, orange eyes casting furtive glances toward the cavalcade of horses that quickly moved from a walk to a trot, and then kicked up to a ground eating canter. They were hopeful of distancing themselves from the wolves before they could cross the ravine.

19 / Pack

Ezra lay along the neck of his bay, black mane whipping his face, but he was aiming for a cluster of trees at the edge of the ravine, hoping they could keep the horses contained in the trees while they fought off the wolves. Weaving in and out and around the sage, cacti, and rocks, he led the way to where the bank of the ravine had caved in and offered a way to the trees. They bounded down the sloping bank with horses in tow and fought slapping branches to get into the midst of the cottonwoods and willows, swinging down before the horses slid to a stop. Both men had rifles and saddle pistols in hand and quickly dropped behind a downed cottonwood, looking for the wolves.

Gabe lay the two saddle pistols on the rough bark of the dead tree, lay the fore stock of the Ferguson on the trunk and searched for a target. But the blackness of the ravine was more of an advantage for the wolves with their dark coats. Suddenly one leaped out of the black, fangs bared, eyes blazing, and Gabe only had time to thrust the muzzle of the rifle forward and pull the trigger. The blast racketed in the close confines, and the blaze of the muzzle flared as the chest of the wolf impacted the muzzle. The big lead ball tore a massive hole in the wolf's chest and a larger one in his back as it exited. The bitter smell of ignited powder mixed with burnt hair assailed their nostrils and the carcass of the black wolf fell before the log.

Gabe quickly dropped the Ferguson beside him and snatched up a .62 caliber saddle pistol. He was hopeful he had not erred with his thinking, for he had loaded the pistols heavy and double-shotted them, hoping to do more damage to his target than to his wrist as he fired. After his scare with the cougar, he was determined to be better prepared. He searched for another target but the roar from Ezra's Lancaster Rifle snapped his head around and he saw another pair of orange eyes and the grey wolf stagger, still snarling. He tried to lunge at Ezra, but Gabe dropped the hammer on his saddle pistol and the big gun bucked in his hand, emitting smoke, fire, and lead and the wolf was knocked back and down.

Ezra glanced at Gabe, "What was that?"

"Loaded 'em heavy and double," answered Gabe as he brought the second hammer to full cock, looking for another wolf.

A scream and a crash of breaking branches came from behind them and Gabe jumped to his feet, hollered back to Ezra, "Stay here!" and ran into the trees. He was met with a flying fur ball that had been launched with the hind legs of Ebony and the heavy weight of the wolf carcass knocked him to his back. The beast struggled to his feet, staggered and turned to face Gabe just as the man got to his knees. Before the big grey predator of the wilderness could take a step, Gabe fired the second barrel of his saddle pistol and the double impact took the grey to the ground, blood blossoming at his chest and neck, but he was dead before he hit the ground.

Gabe stood, walked to the carcass, poked it with his toe as he put the saddle pistol in his belt and drew his Bailes belt pistol, bringing it to full cock. The wolf was dead, and Gabe walked to the horses, speaking low and calmly, touching each one, reassuring them, but watching the trees and his big black for any danger. Another blast came from Ezra and Gabe turned and ran back to his friend.

"You all right?" he asked as he came from the trees.

"Yeah. Got another'n. How many did you see?"

"Four, I think. If that's all there were, we've gotten 'em all, but let's not take any chances," suggested Gabe as he picked up the Ferguson and started reloading. Ezra had finished reloading his rifle and scanned the area before them for any movement while Gabe finished reloading his pistol. "You go back to the horses, check around there and I'll do a quick look-see around here, then we'll get away from these carcass-es, the horses don't like the smell."

Ezra huffed, "I don't either!"

When the two friends came back together, Gabe said, "You know, we're gonna be spendin' the winter in the mountains, and it gets pretty cold. So, I'm thinkin' the pelts of these wolves could make some good winter coats."

Ezra cocked his head to the side, looked askance at his friend, and answered, "I s'pose you want me to skin them stinkin' things out just so's you'll be nice an' warm come winter?"

"You too! And 'sides, what with my recent near mortal wounds, you can't 'spect me to do it, do you?"

"You think the horses will like packin' those stinkin' hides?"

"No more'n they like packin' the cougar hides you think you snuck into the panniers."

"Hummph," mumbled Ezra as he leaned his rifle against a tree and started toward the nearest carcass, knife in hand.

It took some doing, but both men busied themselves at skinning out the wolf carcasses and soon had the pelts ready to salt down. They rolled them tight with several bunches of crushed sage to mask the wild smell, wrapped them in a ground cover and had them ready for loading. But they first repacked the rest of the gear, distributing it among all three pack horses.

Although their plan had been to travel at night, the eastern sky showed heavy dark clouds with bright pink underbellies before they were finished with their task. Choosing to continue their trek anyway, they loaded the fresh pelts on the little sorrel, believing she would be easier to handle and less likely to get spooked. Although once she got a whiff of the cargo, she crow-hopped around in a tight circle with Ezra hanging on to the lead rope, but she soon settled down and was ready for the trail.

It was mid-afternoon when they came to the confluence of the Medicine Bow River and the North Platte River. They had kept to the south of the Medicine Bow since leaving the mountains, following the suggested route from Black Eagle and although they didn't know the rivers by the names they would later be known as, they recognized landmarks spoken of by Eagle and had made their journey without difficulty. The horses, including the mustangs, had become used to the undulating plains with the many ravines and gullies they had to cross, but the adobe and sandy soil was easy traveling and they made good time.

"Let's move back upstream a little, it looks like the shoulder drops off into the river bottom and there's some cottonwoods that look good," suggested Gabe. The two days in the saddle were showing their wear on him and he was looking forward to a day or two of rest. He reined Ebony to the left and clucked him forward to what appeared as a trail off the knoll and down the shoulder slope. When he came to the trail, he reined up, leaning to one side for a better look at the ground below. He stepped down, went to one knee to examine his findings, and lifted his eyes to Ezra, "Looks like Indian ponies, no more'n five. Tracks look to be at least a day old and going down to the bottom. They might still be down there."

Ezra had come close up behind him and leaned over for a look-see. "Maybe I should go down first, see what's there."

Gabe stood, looked from Ezra to the valley floor, "With no more'n five or so, shouldn't be a problem. If we go sneakin' up on 'em they might think we're trouble. Let's just go ready for bear." Gabe swung back aboard, checked his saddle pistols, loosened the Ferguson in the scabbard, and nodding to Ezra, started to the trail.

The path was rocky, and the five horses' hooves clattered with every step, doing little to mask their approach, but that was fine with Gabe, he wanted whoever was down there to know they were coming. The trail bottomed out and Gabe pointed Ebony to the grove of cottonwoods, thinking if anyone was here, that would the site of their camp. They drew close to the trees and an arrow whispered past Gabe's head prompting him to instantly snatch the Ferguson from the scabbard as he dropped to the ground, wincing at the pain, but focused on the trees that harbored the arrow shooter. He hunched behind a rock and brought the Ferguson to bear on the tree line, then hollered, "We're peaceful! Don't mean no harm!"

But no answer came nor did any more arrows. Gabe twisted to see Ezra, also scrunched down behind a small brush, then looked again to the trees. He called out, "We're gettin' up and comin' in!"

Again, there was no answer, and Gabe slowly rose, holding his left hand high, the right holding the Ferguson at his side. He backstepped to Ebony, stepped aboard and slid the rifle into the scabbard, nodded to Ezra and watched the trees for any movement while Ezra mounted. Ezra whispered to Gabe, "I'll hold back a ways, don't wanna be too close to make it easy on 'em. Keep your hand on your saddle pistol or hold it on your lap, don't know what we're gettin' into!"

Gabe already had one of the big over/under double barreled saddle pistols cradled in his lap as he gigged the horse forward. He let the clatter of hooves on rocks mask the sound of bringing both hammers to full cock. The big black moved with tentative steps, ears forward, head high and nostrils flaring. Gabe could feel the tense manner of the stallion who could also feel that of his master. As they moved into the trees, a clearing opened to reveal a picket line of five horses, a hide tipi, a cookfire circle with smoldering coals under a simmering pot, and a girl of about fourteen standing beside a boy of about twelve who held a bow with nocked arrow at his side. Both were scowling at the visitors as they approached, but neither moved.

20 / Shoshoni

Gabe and Ezra sat immobile, watching the two that stood before the hide tipi. Finally, Gabe broke the silence, "We are friends," using sign and speaking in the language that was common to the Arapaho, Pawnee, and Omaha. Although each of those tribes had their own dialect, the base language was similar enough that most could understand. But he received only blank looks from the two, until the girl, using sign, responded.

"Are you alone?" she asked.

"Yes, and we mean you no harm," replied Gabe. "May I get down?"

"Yes, but leave your weapons."

Gabe nodded, looked to Ezra and both men stepped down. Gabe dropped Ebony's reins to ground tie the big horse and signed to the girl, "Are you all right?" He had detected a mood or expression that told him something was wrong. These two youngsters should not be alone and there were five horses, but no one else appeared nearby.

"There's has been sickness. It has taken some of my family."

"Is your village close?"

"No, five or six days, in the Wind River mountains," signed the girl.

"Why are you alone?" questioned Gabe.

"Because of the sickness. Others had it and died, we were to stay behind until we became well or . . ." she responded, dropping her eyes.

"How many of your family did it take?" asked Gabe.

"My father and mother and a brother."

Gabe shook his head, looked at Ezra and back at the girl. "Are you and your brother sick also?"

"No, it has been three days since my family was taken. We buried them and their blankets and more with them."

Ezra spoke softly to Gabe, "Sure wish I knew what sickness, we could get it if these two have it but just haven't come down with it yet."

"I don't think so. They look healthy enough and with it bein' three days past, I think they're alright," surmised Gabe.

"Do you know what sickness?" he asked the girl.

"Yes. The spotted sickness of the white man. A trader and his woman visited our village before we left on the buffalo hunt, and she took sick before we left. Then others became sick with it."

Gabe looked at Ezra, "Smallpox!" muttered Gabe, catching the glimpse from Ezra. They both shook their heads, looked around at the camp, and turned back to the girl.

"You did right in burying the things with your family. But anything they touched should be burned, even the lodge and more."

The girl's eyes flashed wide, looked back at the lodge and what she could see inside, then at her brother. "But it is all we have."

"You have your life; and that is more important than anything else. If you don't act now, you will come down sick and join your family. We will help you, but it must be done immediately!"

The girl turned to her brother who had stepped back and slightly raised the bow and arrow toward the two intruders, but the girl stood before him and vigorously argued with the boy, pleading for him to allow the things to be destroyed. He continued to resist, but she stepped closer and forced the bow down as she stood before him and spoke in softer tones. Finally, she turned around and asked, "What do we do?"

"First, I am Gabe, and this is Ezra," he spoke the names aloud so she could hear how they were pronounced, then continued, "He will take some blankets down to the river." He went to his bedroll and brought out a bar of lye soap and handed it to her. "You and your brother go to the river, scrub really hard everywhere with this, then wrap up in the blankets and come back. We will tend to things here. When you've taken your clothes off, toss them aside and we'll burn them too."

The two friends knew not to touch anything and chose to

use long sticks to handle what needed to be done. Everything that was scattered about, blankets, willow backrest, moccasins, and other miscellaneous items as well as all the robes, pads, parfleches and more in the tipi had to be destroyed. By throwing everything in the tipi and using firebrands from the cookfire, the conflagration of smallpox was soon spiraling upwards in a twisting column of smoke. The brother and sister returned as the tall lodgepoles of the tipi crashed down sending a greater cloud of smoke and embers flying. They stood wide-eyed, watching until Gabe spoke.

"We need to cross the river and put some distance between us and this. If there's anyone near, they would see that and come investigate. I'd just as soon be gone as to have another problem to deal with."

"I agree with that!" declared Ezra and went to the horses. The girl, who they discovered was named Singing Bird, pointed the way to a good crossing of the bigger river that stretched about a hundred feet wide, but was no more than three feet at its deepest. Bird and her brother, Badger Tail, led their spare horses and crossed first, closely followed by Gabe leading the sorrel and Ezra leading the mustangs. The valley bottom had an abundance of old-growth cottonwood and several thickets of chokecherries, buffalo berries, and more. They moved a couple miles downstream to distance themselves from the smoke and with daylight fading, made camp in the trees.

Gabe stripped the gear from the horses as Ezra started gathering wood for a cook fire. Badger Tail tended their horses, picketing them on some grass near the riverbank and Bird gravitated to Ezra, and helped with the fire, believing she would be expected to do the cooking. She was surprised when Ezra set about cutting some steaks from the last of the venison and hung them over the fire to start broiling. He began mixing some batter for cornmeal biscuits and she volunteered to take over. Ezra smiled, handed her the pan and picked up the coffee pot to fetch some water for coffee.

The mood during their meal was a little somber, conversation difficult with their hands full of food. Bird and Badger Tail had fashioned their trade blankets, poncho style, with a slit in the middle for their head and the rest tied at their waist. They were comfortable but asked Gabe about other clothes to which he was only able to answer, "We'll get you some deerskin just as soon as we can. Do you know how to tan 'em?"

"Yes. If we have the hides, I can make the clothes," explained Bird. "But it will take time."

"How far are we from the Sweetwater?" asked Gabe.

Bird's brow furrowed as she asked, "You know of the Sweetwater?"

"Yes. I was told about it. Would that be a good place to stop and prepare hides and more?"

She nodded as she signed, "It is a good place. Two days away."

With an early start, they moved almost directly west, following a little creek that snaked through the valley floor with a long ridge of mountains rising almost two thousand feet higher off their right shoulder. Bird was riding beside Gabe as they followed Ezra and Badger Tail and he turned to the girl, pointed at the mountains and asked, "What are they called?"

She smiled, "The Painted Mountains. Those stripes are like the sign after the rain, but different."

Gabe turned to look directly at the long ridge that made him think of the spine of some long animal. With evenly spaced finger ridges coming from the taller ridge, the colors of the soil danced over each break as if painted with a multi-colored brush in the shaky hands of the Creator. Each stripe differed in width as well as color with the lowest one a pale tan, with a broader stripe of pale orange riding the ridges above it. A broad stripe of brighter orange danced atop the lower one but was intermittent in its stroke. Then a banner of tan, sprinkled with the dark green of piñon trees, waved across the ridges and was crowned with a wide stripe of white. Below it all the darker soil of the low shoulders showed an odd mix of deep maroon with splotches of green meadows and some splattered white alkali. Gabe shook his head in wonder, but his attention was captured when Bird said as she signed, "At the end of the ridge is a cut through these mountains to the Sweetwater. We should camp in the cut this night. There will be deer there."

Gabe knew she was thinking both of food and the skins to make her and her brother some buckskins, and he smiled as he thought of this girl being so responsible as to be thinking of her brother and herself as well and how to take care of their needs. Most youngsters this age would only be thinking about what kind of mischief they could get into or game they could play, not anything as basic as food and clothing. But the way of the wilderness aged many before their time.

21 / Hides

They had no sooner stripped the gear from the horses and started their usual preparations for making camp, when Bird came from the creek carrying a big bundle of willows. Both men stood agape as she dropped the load, grinning, then went to her knees and started fashioning drying racks for smoking meat. Gabe said as he signed, "We don't have any meat to dry, yet."

Birdlookedupathim,smiled,andsigned,"Thengogetsome. I saw some deer at the creek. Or do I have to get them myself?" Gabe looked at Ezra who was busy with the firewood preparing a cookfire, "Guess I've been given my orders. I'll be back directly," he declared as he went to his gear to get his bow and quiver. When Bird saw him coming from his gear with the quiver and case, she asked, "Where is your rifle?"

"Won't need it. I'm taking my bow," he replied, holding the case up for her to see. She frowned, and watched as he walked away, then returned to the racks. As he passed, he glanced at Badger Tail and motioned for him to come along and bring his bow. The boy quickly snatched up his bow and trotted behind Gabe until he stopped to string his bow. The boy watched, fascinated with the weapon and the difficulty Gabe had in stringing the bow, but marveled as he saw it strung and ready. But the boy, though curious and full of questions, remained mum and followed Gabe as they went to the edge of the willows and started upstream on the grassy bank.

Within a short distance, Gabe dropped down to one knee, pointing to the shallow grassy draw that emptied into the creek where eight deer grazed, some nearer the creek but all working their way to the water for their evening drink. One big buck that still had a strip of velvet hanging from his rack, stood watch over his harem, but often dropped his head for graze. Two other bucks, one a fork-horn, the other a spike, grazed nearer the others. Two older does had fawns by their side, and one doe, probably last year's fawn, was at the water.

Gabe pointed to the larger of the two young bucks and motioned for Badger Tail to take it. Gabe had an arrow nocked as did the boy, and he waited as the boy carefully moved ahead, staying beside the willows and moving only when the deer were grazing or looking elsewhere. Within moments, he was in position and slowly stood, bringing his bow to full draw as he did, then he stepped away from the willows and let his arrow fly. The shaft quivered as it flew to its mark and buried itself deep in the chest of the buck. The buck staggered, swung around and started to follow the herd buck back to the tree-covered hills. He stumbled, staggered, and fought to stay on his feet. The big does and their fawns had spooked at the sudden movement of the bucks and in great bounds, their fawns at their sides, they passed the stumbling buck, just as he fell on his neck, kicking and bleating for an instant, then fell still.

Gabe had picked his targets as the younger buck and the young doe, and stood where he was, arrow nocked and ready. When Badger Tail released his arrow, Gabe's followed and within an instant of the boy's arrow striking, Gabe's arrow impaled the younger buck and the impact drove him to the ground where he kicked several times, trying to get to his feet, but quickly stopped, sightless eyes staring at the fleeing does. The young doe had leaped over the downed buck, but Gabe's second arrow caught her in flight and her legs buckled as they hit the ground and she fell in a heap, unmoving.

When the doe fell, Badger Tail turned back to look at Gabe who was about fifteen yards behind him, then looked at the doe and back at Gabe. He shook his head as he started to his buck and knelt beside the carcass to begin dressing it out. Gabe walked up behind him, put his hand on his shoulder then signed as he spoke, "You did well. That was a good shot." The boy looked at Gabe, twisted around on his haunches and signed, "I never saw a white man before. I did not know you used a bow and you took two deer. The doe was jumping high when you shot it." It was obvious from the boy's expression that he was quite impressed with Gabe's use of the bow and wanted to say more but turned back to his work.

When Badger Tail finished gutting his deer, Gabe sent him back to camp for a horse to pack the deer out and continued with his work on the doe. When the boy returned with two horses, Gabe hefted the carcass of the smaller buck and the doe on the first horse and the other deer on the second. They returned to camp, where Bird waited by the trees, Gabe's riata in hand, ready to hang the carcasses to make it easy for skinning and stripping the meat.

It was a busy night, but with all four working diligently, the deer were soon skinned, the meat deboned, and while Gabe and Ezra started cutting the meat in thin strips for smoking, Bird and Badger Tail took the hides to the stream. Bird had scooped out a small pool in a sandbar and put the hides underwater, weighing them down with rocks to thoroughly soak. She returned to the camp and went to the fire and scooped up some of the ashes on a flat rock and started back toward the stream, but stopped and sat the rock down and signed as she spoke, "When you can, come to the stream and fill the pool with the hides with your urine." She picked up the rock with the ashes and turned away to go to the pool.

Gabe chuckled, and turned back to his task of cutting strips of meat for smoking. They both knew that the acid of urine was commonly used in the tanning of hides, but it was just the way she said it, without any regard for their response or reaction. They both shook their heads and resumed their work, chuckling.

"Maybe it's just a woman thing. You know, it seems to come natural to 'em to give us men orders," remarked Ezra, still cutting at the meat.

"Maybe so, but can you imagine what she'll be like when she grows into a woman and marries up with some buck? He'll have to swaller his pride mighty quick if he wants a peaceable home."

"Well, one thing for sure, we'll have us a bunch o' smoked meat for our journey!"

"Yeah, she said these three," nodding to the deer carcasses, "were a good start but she would need several more. So, like I said, I guess I've got my orders."

"Well, I reckon she is a little tired of wearin' that blanket for clothes. I'd probably be wantin' some new buckskins too."

"You? What about me? That lion ripped that other set to shreds!" He motioned to the outfit he wore, "This is my last set!"

"Well, yeah. But if that cougar hadn't done that, we wouldn't have had all those buckskin strips to bandage you up with, so, every cloud has its silver lining!"

Gabe shook his head as he chuckled at Ezra. "Shore didn't feel like no cloud!"

It was noon of the following day when they reached the Sweetwater River. After coming through the notch between the mountain ridges, they followed the small creek into the flats and as the rocky hills rose before them, the Sweetwater painted the valley bottom with a wide swath of green. They crossed the stream, water so clear they could see the trout swimming against the current and the gravely bottom that offered sure footing for the horses. The cold water was no more than three feet at its deepest, but the current was swift, and the horses leaned against it as they crossed.

They pitched their camp at the base of the rocky hillside and with the hill at their backs, the juniper and piñon offered additional windbreaks as the prevailing wind came from off the mountains and the canyon that was carved by the Sweetwater. No sooner had they stopped than Bird was at the stream's edge, and soon began scooping out another pool for the hides where the stream bent back on itself in a horseshoe bend, leaving a broad sandbar for her worktable.

Bird often giggled as she watched Gabe, Ezra and her brother busy at the tasks she had assigned them. Although all three took the time in early morning and late evening to replenish their store of deer hides, during the day she had given brief instructions then put them to work. Gabe was scraping hides with the dried scapula bone of one of the deer to rid them of any flesh or membrane, while Ezra was stretching the treated hides over the smooth edge of a big flat rock that stood erect for the task. Badger Tail was applying the brain slurry to the scraped hides and erecting the smoking lodge for treating the finished hides. Bird looked at the men, busy at their tasks, and smiled, knowing what they were doing would never be seen in their village, for all this was women's work and men would never stoop to such tasks.

As they worked, she went to a large flat rock, picked up her small round stone, and began pounding the dried sinew taken from the back-strap ligaments and the hind leg ligaments of the deer, preparing to make the sinew thread to be used in sewing the garments. She had found a large ball of pitch on the side of a ponderosa, and would use the pitch to treat the sinew, making it waterproof for the clothing. Tomorrow, the third day of their stay on the Sweetwater, she would begin cutting and sewing and would soon have comfortable clothing for herself and her brother.

22 / Sweetwater

It had been over a week since they stopped at the Sweetwater and now, they were finally ready to start back on their journey to the Wind River Mountains and the village of the Shoshoni. Bird was in her fringed dress with a fine line of beadwork at the yoke, long fringe dangling from the short sleeves, yokes, and hem. Badger Tail was proud of his new leggings, fringe at the seam, and a new breechcloth with a geometric pattern of diamonds in beads at the front. Bird was still working on a tunic for her brother, but everyone was anxious to be back on the move. Where they had camped was at a junction of the hunting lands of the Cheyenne, Crow, Arapaho, and Shoshoni, and although they were not at war with one another, they weren't all that friendly either. And the party of four people and ten horses would make quite a prize for any band of raiders.

Gabe and Ezra had learned a lot from the girl. She had walked them through the tanning of the wolf and cougar hides, and they had succeeded in making nice soft pelts that could be used in the making of winter clothing when needed. And all were learning the language of the other as they shared in the daily labors. Gabe and Bird now rode alongside one another and seemed to be constantly talking and learning each other's language, both laughing at the other as they tried to pronounce difficult and strange words. Yet, Bird seemed to be learning English much faster than either Gabe or Ezra was picking up Shoshoni.

They didn't have an early start on their first day on the trail with their new duds and as the afternoon wore on they were traveling into the sun. By staying on the south side of the Sweetwater, they avoided the serpentine trail on the north that hugged the hillsides, and the travel was easy. But an upthrust of rocky knolls along the bank where the river turned north, steered them away from the water and into the flats. However, Bird pointed in the distance and assured them they would meet up with the river after it bent back to the west.

The bright sun hung suspended from the canopy of blue and dared them to continue into its glare when Gabe pointed to a cluster of massive rock hills and said, "Let's make camp there. It's close to the water and should have good cover."

Bird smiled and said, "Those are called the Sweetwater Rocks."

"They're rocks alright, solid rock!" declared Gabe as he pointed Ebony to a cut that appeared to provide entry into the maze. They rode between two low rounded ridges, each about a thousand feet long and fifty feet high at their peak, that made Gabe think of massive ancient dinosaurs buried in the dirt and petrified. He grinned at his foolish thought and lifted his eyes to the massive knobs before him that rose well over five hundred feet from the valley floor. When he declared they were solid rock, he didn't realize how true his assumption was until they drew near. They appeared as solid stone, marked by narrow cracks and splits, with scattered cedar bushes and piñon trees tenuously clinging to what soil had drifted into the cracks and gave toeholds to germinated seeds long ago.

Worn by eons of wild Rocky Mountain winds and storms, the smooth granite harbored untold stories of ancient creatures and peoples that would never be heard. Cradled within the cluster of stone was a sloping grassless flat, marred by alkali and drifted tumbleweeds. Gabe chose a horseshoe shaped hollow with bunched piñon near the entry for their camp site. There were signs of prior use, probably by hunting parties of the Shoshoni or others. Because of the slope behind, the occasional runoff water had given ample moisture for a sizable patch of grass that would not have been seen without entering the cul-de-sac. Gabe stepped down, dropping the reins to ground tie Ebony and helped the others with the extra horses.

He looked at Ezra with a frown and spoke softly, "Dunno what it is, but my hackles are up and I got this feelin' . . ."

"Me too. I've been lookin' around and ain't seen nuthin', but . . ."

"I think I'll shinny up atop this knob behind us and have a look-see," said Gabe, slipping his brass telescope from the saddlebags.

"Sing out if you see sumpin'!"

"You know I will," answered Gabe as he slipped the Ferguson from the scabbard. He checked the loads and started to the rocks to work his way up. He soon found it required both hands and feet on the smooth rock, even though the cracks and uneven surface seemed to offer footholds, the surface was deceiving, and he had to slip the sling over his head and shoulder to hold his rifle and make the climb.

Using a couple of cedar bushes for cover, he lay down on the sun-warmed rock between them and stretched out the scope. He faced north, wanting to scan the flat that showed between some rocky mounds across the Sweetwater. He had learned to pay attention to his senses and the feeling that there was trouble near had seemed to crawl up his back like a cold shiver. He breathed deep and rested his arm on the rock, steadying the scope and searched the flats for movement. The flats were barren, scattered clumps of sage, patches of cacti, bunch grass, but nothing moving. Then suddenly a puff of dust and he spotted four, five pronghorn antelope stretching out and running from something. They disappeared behind some rocks and Gabe swung the scope back just in time to see several mounted warriors come from behind a low rise and moving toward the Sweetwater. He guessed them to be maybe two miles distant, and if they continued their way and crossed the river, they would soon be upon them. But if Gabe and company moved now, they would certainly be seen. He kept the scope on the group, counting sixteen warriors. Although they trailed a pair of packhorses, there was nothing to show they were hunting or that there might be a village nearby.

"What do you see?" came a whisper from behind him.

Gabe jerked at the voice and turned to see Bird sitting on her heels behind him. She was obscured from view by the brush, but he had not expected anyone to follow him up the rock and she had silently approached him without his awareness. He motioned her down beside him, pointed in the distance and said, "That looks like a raiding party of some kind. I can't determine who they are, but you can have a look. Maybe you'll know." He handed her the scope, watched her frown and carefully hold it, but a question showed in her eyes, so he helped her.

"Here, like this," he demonstrated. "It will help you see them."

He handed it back to her and she mimicked his movements, then jerked back from the scope, looked at it and at Gabe, prompting Gabe to chuckle. "It's alright, take another look, move it until you see the band of warriors."

She gave it another try, slowly peering into the scope then moving it around. It was obvious when she saw the mounted warriors, causing her to frown and say, "Those are Haih! They call themselves the Apsáslooke, or the Black Bird People." She spat the words and added, "They are our enemy! They come for horses and captives!"

"Do you mean they are the Crow?" asked Gabe.

She lowered the scope, looked at it closely and handed it back to Gabe. "Yes, the Crow!" She looked toward the raiding party and saw how far away they were, then turned to Gabe, "They are fierce warriors. They have attacked my people before and taken many scalps and captives."

"Then you slip off and go tell Ezra we need to be ready to leave in a hurry. I'll stay and watch them a few more minutes, they might make camp 'fore they get too close."

Bird nodded, and slid back from the bushes, and took a route down the rock that kept her on the far side from the approaching raiders. When she trotted back into camp, she quickly told Ezra and Badger, using sign and newly learned words, about the impending danger. They immediately set to work re-rigging the horses to ready them for travel. Although none of them liked being geared up again, they had enjoyed a few moments of graze and water and would be good for a few more miles. Within moments, Gabe slid from the last hump of rock and came near, "Looks like they're makin' camp. They're still on the other side of the river and I think the water'll mask any noise we make, but I think we should try to wait until full dark 'fore we move out. One of us will have to stay near the horses, try to keep 'em from whinnying to those across the river, but I think they'll be alright."

"So, we get to travel by moonlight," commented Ezra.

Gabe chuckled, "Ummhmmm, at least for tonight. But the moon is waxing to about half, so with a clear night we'll be able to see good 'nuff." Ezra had not started a fire yet, so Bird dug out some of their fresh smoked venison and a handful of left-over johnnycakes and they bided their time, watching the far shore from behind a shoulder of the big mound.

The Crow made camp on the west edge of a big rock knob that sloped off toward their camp. With less than fifty yards to the river below, it gave them high ground and a good promontory for scouting the countryside. They had two small cookfires and the horses were picketed near the river giving them grass and water with two men standing watch. As Gabe looked, he knew they could see him as clearly as he saw them, even though their camp was close to a mile away, and he stayed well behind the rock. Yet as the dusk faded into darkness, he also saw the two warriors by the horses had both found a comfortable spot and were partially reclined as they tended the animals. As he watched, movement atop the rock caught his attention and he saw a lookout moving about, probably searching for some place of comfort for the night. As he gazed, Gabe considered their position in relation to the Crow and what they would have to do to get away. Although the half-moon would provide light for them to ride, that same illumination would make it easier to be seen by the Crow. He turned around to look at their position, calculating the possible escape route, then grinned as he pictured their moves.

He walked back to the others, and spoke to Ezra first, "You will lead off, trailing the mustangs, and go back through the cut. But, once out of the cut, go straight south toward the hills yonder. There's a draw that comes from the notch with what looked like a small creek. It's probably three, four miles. Head that way, keeping these rocks at your back and if the rest of us don't catch up by the time you get to the hills, wait for us."

Ezra nodded, "But if I hear shootin', I'm comin' back!"

"I'd expect you to do just that. But hopefully, you won't." He turned to Badger and Bird, "Bird, you'll lead two of your spare horses, and follow Ezra, but wait till he's gone from the cut before you start. And Badger, you'll lead your other pack horse and follow her, but space it out. Too many together make too much noise. Then I'll follow once I know you've made it clear." He looked to each of the others, received nods of agreement, then stepped back and said to Ezra, "See ya soon!" and watched as he rode from the cut.

23 / Surprise

They kept a steady gait, moving due west across the buffalo grass flat. The half-moon was joined by a clear night full of stars and they made good progress. With a middle of the night stop at a wide ravine with a small creek in the bottom, they gave the horses a breather and risked a small fire for coffee and meat and biscuits heated in the flat pan. Gabe looked at Bird and asked, "You said the Sweetwater bends back to the south and we should cross it 'fore too long, is that right?"

"Yes. It is not far now," she answered, passing out the hot biscuits with smoked meat.

"So, we should make it 'fore daylight?"

She looked to the sky, judging the time and answered, "Yes."

"Good. Then if there's trees and such, we'll camp there for the day, let the horses get some rest and graze

"Our village is less than a day from there."

Gabe glanced at the girl, surprised they were that close to

their village. "Do you think the Crow are looking for your village?"

"Yes. The buffalo have gone north or into the valley of the Wind River. They will not go south until later. That is when the Crow use the buffalo jumps to take their winter meat. If they were hunting, they would not be here, but in the mountains where there are elk, deer, and sheep. Here there is mostly pronghorn, and little meat on them. That is a raiding party after horses and captives. The young warriors want honors in battle and horses to trade for women for their lodge. Some will take captives from raids to take as their wives."

Gabe looked at Ezra and back at Bird, "So, they might be following us to let us take them to the village?"

"Yes, or if they do not know we," nodding to her brother, "are with you, they would follow just to take the horses. If their scouts saw us, they would follow just to take that one," pointing to Ebony.

Ezra shrugged, "See, you just can't help it. Either you find a damsel in distress, or some outlaw or Indian wants your horse! No matter what, we are always in some kind of predicament! You attract trouble like stink draws flies!"

Gabe chuckled, knowing his friend wasn't complaining as much as observing, "Admit it, life would be boring without me! You couldn't stand it!"

Ezra chuckled, shaking his head, "I dunno. Sometimes I think I'd like to give it a try. But you're right, I'd probably die of boredom!"

"Well, let's push on to the river and decide then just what we'll do," suggested Gabe.

The dim grey of early morning allowed them to find a well-used campsite on the west bank of the Sweetwater River. After crossing the shallow waters, their chosen camp held alders, willows and a few cottonwoods giving the horses both shelter and graze and the tree cover protected the sleepers from discovery. But Gabe was restless and after a couple hours of fidgety sleep, he rose from the blankets and with rifle and scope in hand, mounted the ridge that shadowed the river and offered a significant promontory for viewing their back trail.

As he scanned the flats with his scope, he thought of the Crow and if they were following, how long they might have before they came. He searched the north bank and the terrain along the river, then the flats to the south. He was certain that if they were bent on taking horses, they would have found their tracks and know they were not far behind. The dry country was prone to dust storms and an occasional dust devil was common, and he watched as a pair of them danced across the flat, twisting their way toward the foothills. He saw a small bunch of pronghorns grazing and lazily moving toward the river, but nothing else moved.

Then a brief flash of light caught his attention and he turned the scope to the ridge on the north bank. There it was again, and a thin trail of dust rising lazily above the ridge. He focused on the spot, adjusting the long brass barrel of the scope, and could barely make out a group of riders moving atop the rimrock lined ridge. But the group wasn't as large as what he had seen the day before, maybe half the size, about seven or eight riders. And what was it that caught the sun? Most of the natives seldom wore anything that had the brightness to reflect the sun, but he had known them to trade for geegaws such as Mexican conchos, or hand mirrors from the French, and sometimes these would be used as decoration for coup sticks or war shields or even on clothing.

For good measure, he looked away from the first group and searched the flats again. If their tracks had been found, they would probably have someone following the same route they traveled across the flats. And there they were, just coming out of the wide ravine that had served as their temporary camp for the midnight breather for the horses. So, they had split to two groups, now what? He watched both groups a moment longer, then backed off the ridge and dropped down to return to camp.

Ezra was heating up the coffee and munching on a johnnycake and looked up at Gabe as he walked back into camp. He could tell by his friend's expression that trouble was coming. "How long?"

"Maybe a couple hours," answered Gabe. "They split into two groups. One is following the ridge north of the river, the other following our trail."

"So, no mistakin' they're after us," surmised Ezra. "Got a plan?"

Gabe looked up as both Bird and Badger came from their

blankets. They had heard his remarks and wanted to hear the rest. He nodded to them, and began, "I'm thinkin' booby traps!"

Ezra chuckled, "That's different."

"What are 'booby traps'?" asked Bird, coming nearer.

"It's kinda hard to explain," he started, but began to try as he told about the times he and Ezra had often set traps for one another when they were in the woods as youths.

"But, that won't stop them," pleaded Bird.

"No, but it might make 'em afraid, that is, if we do all we can."

After an additional explanation, he saw the understanding and ideas paint the faces of his listeners as they slowly grinned. Both Bird and Badger volunteered to help and took off on their assigned tasks. Ezra and Gabe went to their packs to get as many rawhide and buckskin strips as they had and started setting their traps.

They knew the two groups would approach the camp from the common trails that led to the river crossing. The band from the flats would probably follow their tracks to the crossing and the ridge riders would take the easiest trail into the trees. The traps were set accordingly and once complete, Gabe thought they had less than an hour before the bands arrived and he sent Bird and Badger with all the extra horses ahead to warn their village of the possible attack. As they watched to two leave, they looked at one another, grinned and Gabe said, "Let's find us a spot up the trail in that gulley for the last trap."

They mounted up and followed the trail used by Bird and Badger and searched for good cover to launch their attack. "I'll take the ridge so I can send them the first message," stated Gabe, pointing to the rocks at the rim. Ezra answered, "Over there looks like a good spot," he pointed at a stack of rocks that pushed out into the ravine floor and had a scraggly piñon near the pinnacle. Gabe nodded and started away, turned back, "Keep your head down!"

Ezra chuckled, "You're the one that needs to do that, compadre."

Gabe had bellied down atop the ridge and positioned himself to watch the camp with the telescope. They had left a small fire in the middle of the camp and put green branches on the coals to give plenty of smoke to make the raiders believe they were still there. The band from the ridge dropped into the river bottom and spread out a little, working their way through the trees and brush. Gabe had assumed some would stay mounted and he watched the trail for the first trap. Suddenly a whinny and scream from a horse and rider split the quiet, the horse reared up, pawing at the sky, and fell backwards on his rider. Gabe chuckled and whispered, "Good job, Ezra!" He knew the first trap was two rattlesnakes caught by Badger and hung by their tails from a cottonwood branch over the trail. Gabe had refused to touch the snakes, having no appreciation for the reptiles, but he laughed as he pictured the fright they gave the rider and his horse.

Gabe turned his scope to the lower trail and watched the

band spread out before entering the brush. Within seconds, a scream came from the brush when a trip cord launched a bent over alder that held a loosely tied bull snake. He couldn't tell where it landed, but it certainly scared somebody. The other traps were less dramatic, but effective none the less. From trip cord snares that caught warriors around the ankles and jerked their feet from under them making them crash face first into a bog, to bent branches that when sprung did nothing more than slap a rider from his horse or spook a horse, to shallow but covered holes that brought horse and rider to their knees. The traps, though few, were enough to put the nerves of the attackers on edge and wary of every step and move, fearful of some other trap that might kill or maim them. Gabe chuckled as he heard screams, shouts, taunts, and thrashing through the brush by the angry warriors whose pride had been robbed from them.

The entire band, those still able now numbering thirteen, assembled in the camp and soon rallied to pursue their prey. They started from the trees on the trail in the ravine bottom but went less than twenty yards when the leaders reined up, their horses skittish and sidestepping as they looked at the obstacle in the path. A weathered white buffalo skull, one horn missing, lay staring with empty eyes at the band, a bold red 'x' marking the head. Behind the skull stood crossed poles, decorated with colored ribbon that fluttered in the breeze, several notched feathers flapping at the ends of the ribbon. The movement alarmed the horses and riders as well, but then they heard a high-pitched scream coming from high above. Warriors and horses stared wide-eyed at the sky as a whistling arrow came from Gabe's bow screaming from far away, speeding through the air with a wavering shriek, unable to be seen as it sped toward them.

Two horses broke loose at a run. One then buried his head between his front legs and planted hooves in the ground, bending in the middle and launching his rider overhead to crumble in a screaming heap in a cactus patch. The other started bucking and crow-hopping, the rider holding tight to the mane and squeezing with his legs, unable to stop the runaway. Other horses scattered, some bucking, some running, others side-stepping and tossing their heads trying to unseat their riders so they could flee from the frightening scene.

The young war leader, Hó-ra-tó-a, his long hair hanging in braids down his chest and dangling beside his legs, shouted at his warriors, trying to rally them, but his own horse, skittish as the others, was startled at the shouts and started bucking away from the trail and into the willows by the small creek. Suddenly the leader came unseated and splashed into the water, then stood, shaking a wet fist as his fleeing horse.

Gabe was chuckling at the sight so much, he found it difficult to keep the scope still so he could see. But he knew he had to be ready for they would soon recover and be eager to continue their pursuit. He picked his positions, lay out his saddle pistols, and readied his Ferguson. With patched balls aligned on the flat rock before him, the powder horn sitting ready, everything aligned, he felt he was set.

24 / Skirmish

It was Takes Many Coups who first confronted Hó-ra-tó-a, the war leader of the Crow. Both young men had risen as leaders quickly and often competed with one another to be the chosen leaders of raiding and hunting parties, and although friends, they were also rivals. As the war leader caught up his horse and swung aboard, Takes Many Coups said, "The medicine is bad. We must leave this place."

"My medicine is not bad! If you and the others have lost your nerve, tuck your tails and leave!" spat the war leader. He jerked the head of his horse around and kicked him back to the trail. He pulled up and shouted to the others, "Takes Many Coups thinks my medicine is gone! He has lost his manhood! He will go back to the village with his tail between his legs! Any of you who want to go, GO!"

Without waiting for a response, he yanked his horse around and dug his heels into his ribs, screamed his war cry and started up the trail at a full gallop. He leaned low on the neck of his horse, screaming as he kicked the animal, venting his anger and frustration. He dared not look back to see if any followed, and the sudden barrage of gunfire forced him into the brush at the side of the trail. He leaped from his mount, diving into the buffalo berry bush, frantically looking for cover. The thunder of gunfire continued sporadically, coming from the ridge to his right and the slope on his left. He turned to look back on the trail to see where the others had taken cover and there was no one. He realized he was all alone, facing so many guns, and armed only with his bow and arrows and a lance. He clung to his war shield, trying to see where the shooters were and how many.

Gabe watched as most of the horses spooked and bucked sending many of the riders into the grass and brush alongside the trail. Others, now afoot, took off running after their mounts. Regardless of their situation, facing a band of raiding Crow that would be happy to see him dead, he still had to laugh at the antics of the natives. But he soon gathered himself and made ready for the next act in this drama in the wilderness. He waved at Ezra, who was well situated in the rocks across the ravine floor, their signal to get ready for the attack.

He watched as the raiding party gathered themselves in a bunch beside the trail. The leader was shouting at them, apparently readying them for the attack. But Gabe was surprised to see the leader swing his horse around and charge up the wide ravine by himself. The others hung back and watched. *Well, guess we'll hafta play this out,* he thought as he reached for the saddle pistol and brought it to bear. He wasn't anxious to kill anyone and now that there was just one, he aimed low, firing just one barrel of the pistol and moving quickly to the next saddle pistol and repeating his action, then to the rifle and shooting high. The three blasts were so close to almost sound as one and with Ezra shooting as well, the gunfire and the echoes that bounced back and forth within the high walled ravine made it sound like there were twice as many shooters than expected.

When the war leader dove into the brush, Gabe waved to Ezra to hold his fire and both men quickly reloaded, as they watched the man in the thick brush that showed splotches of pale red where the berries were ripening. He knew the bush had small thorns and wondered just how the war leader was feeling about now. He chuckled and watched, his rifle laying across the flat rock before him, as he kept his sights on the brush. He could easily shoot through the bush as the .52 caliber ball at this range would easily penetrate it, but he waited. He saw a moccasined foot at the edge and he took careful aim, squeezed off his shot and saw the bullet strike at the edge of the foot, that quickly disappeared behind the bush.

Gabe quickly reloaded, keeping his eyes on the bush and saw just the tip of a feather slowly rise above, but a roar from the Lancaster rifle in Ezra's hands, clipped the tip off, eliciting a brief exclamation from the warrior. Gabe chuckled, looked down the trail and saw the dust rising from the retreating warriors that left this one behind. Gabe thought for a moment, then cupped his hands at his mouth and hollered to Ezra. "Hey Ezra! The others left this one behind! He's the only one! Keep him covered. I'm gonna try something!"

Gabe slowly stood, hands held high and shouted down at the war leader. He spoke first in the Algonquian tongue that was common to the Omaha and Pawnee. "Warrior in the brush! Come out and fight, one to one!" There was no response. He tried again in what little he knew of the Siouan tongue common to the Hidatsa and Lakota. Then he tried in the Shoshoni. He knew it was possible he might not be saying things right, but he tried. After each challenge, there was no response.

He held his rifle at his side and slowly descended the slope to the trail, always watching the bush for any movement or possible attempt by the war leader to shoot an arrow. But he did not stir. When Gabe was about thirty yards away, he leaned the rifle against his chest and spoke in English as he signed, "Warrior in the bush! Come out and parley!"

Gabe remained still and watched, rifle again at his side, hammer at full cock and ready to fire. He watched as the war leader slowly stood. The man's face showed a scowl beneath the stiff hair in the pompadour painted white above his forehead. His hair was drawn back in a scalplock that held three feathers, one shortened by Ezra's bullet. Long braids hung over his shoulders covering the beaded buckskin vest. A bone breast plate covered his chest and his leggings showed fringe with feather tufts. The man was not as tall as Gabe, younger and stocky and stood with an arrow nocked in his bow, but not drawn back. He stepped from behind the bush, glowering at Gabe and glancing around to see any other threat. He took a couple of tentative steps forward and watched as Gabe again signed, "We should parley. Your warriors have gone, and you are alone."

Hó-ra-tó-a quickly turned to look at the trail and toward the river, growled as he realized his warriors had left. He looked back to Gabe, then saw Ezra coming from the rocks, rifle held at his shoulder but with the muzzle pointed to the ground. He frowned, making Gabe think he had never seen a black man before. His brow furrowed and he cocked his head slightly as he squinted, then looked back at Gabe.

Gabe signed, "No one has to die today. We can all leave this place alive."

The warrior nodded his head, looking from Gabe to Ezra and back again. Gabe asked, "Why are you here? Were you hunting?"

The man seemed to relax, took the arrow from the bowstring and thrust it into the ground at his side, then leaned the bow against his chest and signed, "I am Hó-ra-tó-a, war leader of the Apsáalooke. We look for horses! You had many!"

Gabe nodded, "Horses are good. But not worth your life. Why did your men leave?"

Hó-ra-tó-a frowned, dropped his eyes and signed, "They believe my medicine was gone."

Gabe knew most native peoples had a strong belief in what they called 'medicine' or the good or bad fortune of a leader. When they have victory, the medicine of the leader is good, but if there are losses and they are defeated, or if hunting and do not take meat, their medicine is bad. Once a leader gets the reputation of bad medicine, it is difficult for him to continue as a leader.

Gabe thought for a moment, "But if you return, unharmed, your medicine will be good."

"Yes. They saw me charge into your guns, saw me leave my horse and think I am dead. To return would be good medicine."

By this time, Ezra was beside Gabe and the war leader kept looking at him, and his curiosity was evident. Then he asked Ezra with sign, "Why do you look like the buffalo?"

Ezra chuckled, leaned his rifle at his chest and answered, "I am called Black Buffalo because of this," he pinched his skin, "and this," he rubbed his hand over his hair, "but there are many like me beyond the big river."

The war leader leaned side to side, looking behind and beyond the two friends, then asked, "How many others are there?"

Gabe chuckled, then signed, "None. Just us."

The warrior looked at their rifles then at the men and said, "There was so much!"

Gabe tapped the pistol at his belt and hefted his rifle, "We can shoot many times. We did not want to kill you, that is why the first shots did not hit you. But when I shot at your foot, and he," nodding to Ezra, "shot your feather, it was to show you we could kill you at any time. This," he tapped his rifle, "would shoot through that bush and kill you."

The war leader looked at Ezra, then at Gabe, and signed, "He is Black Buffalo, what are you called?"

"The Omaha and the Pawnee call me Spirit Bear, or Claw of the Bear."

"I will remember Bear Claw and Black Buffalo. When you are in our lands, tell my people you are friends with Hó-ra-tó-a, and you will be made welcome."

Gabe stretched out his hand as an expression of friendship and the two clasped forearms and the action was repeated by Ezra and the warrior. The two friends watched as Hó-ra-tó-a mounted up and looked at the men, lifted his hand shoulder high, palm forward, then turned and left. Gabe looked at Ezra, "Maybe we made a friend, ya reckon?"

"Humph, I'll believe it when we're in Crow country and don't get scalped!"

"Then maybe we need to gather up our gear and go chase down our pack horses and those two younguns', what say?"

"Lead the way, compadre."

25 / Village

The trail followed a small creek through the wide ravine where even smaller spring fed streams clawed their way down the low hills of the vast basin. They crossed a low saddle to find another small but dry creek bed that pointed to the northeast, winding its way through even more low hills. Gabe noticed a long shoulder that had numerous runoff gullies marking the north slope which he pointed out to Ezra, "Looks like some giant bear clawed that hillside with those gullies all spaced out like that."

"Ummhmm, but what fascinates me is the colors. Look there," pointing to the right, "that hillside has tan, purple, grey, and white. All in stripes, like the Creator just randomly dipped His brush in a whole palette of colors!" He turned to face downstream of the widening ravine, "And look there! That whole valley looks orange or some kinda ochre. And the top o' that mesa yonder is lined with white!"

"It's amazing country, that's for sure," observed Gabe.

And while they were looking up at the hilltops, their horses were suddenly splashing in water and dropping their heads for a drink. Both men stepped down, surprised to see the clear running water where moments before the ravine held nothing but dust and flourishing weeds. Fed by two narrow trickling creeks that came from under the overhanging willows, the water was crystal clear and when they scooped a handful, it was surprisingly cold. "Ummm, that's good!" declared Gabe, scooping another handful and bringing it to his mouth. He doffed his hat and with both hands, brought water to his face and wet fingers through his hair.

Ezra dropped to his belly and buried his face in the cold water, coming up shaking his head side to side and splashing water around. He grinned widely, "Whew! That's cold! I didn't expect it to be that cold!" The water ran down his face and neck and under his collar making him shiver but smile at the refreshing change. Moments before, they had complained about the heat and dust, and this was a welcome change.

They stood and looked down the narrow valley, and Gabe commented, "That's a different sight," nodding to the wide spreading green that showed in the valley bottom. The creek widened, held willows and alders close, but the slight sloping valley showed green. Tall grass waved in the breeze like waves on the sea, two deer jumped from the willows and scampered up the hillside, stopping just before they topped to look back at the intruders and their horses. "The village must be around that bend yonder. Can't be too much further. Singing Bird said it was 'bout a half day from where we camped, so we should be coming to it soon. If it's like this," nodding to the green valley, "It's in a nice place."

They turned to their horses and were startled. Standing beside Ebony was Singing Bird, smiling. "You keep doin' that!" declared Gabe. "Why do you like sneakin' up on me?" The two had developed their own language that was part Shoshoni, part English, part Algonqian, and some sign.

Bird smiled, "It's so easy to do!" she answered.

Gabe shook his head, then looked beyond the girl to see four mounted warriors, less than twenty yards away, watching Bird confront the two friends. Bird nodded toward them, "They are White Knife dog soldiers from my village. There are more, ready for the Apsáalooke. Are they far behind you?"

"Uh, they won't be coming. After the booby traps we set, and more, they decided their medicine was bad and their leader, Hó-ra-tó-a, decided to go back to their people."

Bird motioned to the waiting warriors and one man gigged his horse forward. He was a formidable looking man, broad shouldered, painted for war, long braids hanging beside his bone breast plate and a scalplock that held two feathers. The lower half of his face was painted white, the upper, black, and each cheek had a small yellow lightning bolt. He glared at the two intruders, looked at Bird as she spoke in Shoshoni to tell him what Gabe reported about the Crow. He looked at Gabe, jaw muscles flexing as he ground his teeth, then a slow grin split his face, and he nodded, jerked his horse around to return to the others. His report prompted screams and war cries, as many lifted their war shields or lances as they shouted and laughed at the thought of the Crow fleeing because of bad medicine caused by a young girl and boy. Apparently in the translation, Bird took most of the credit for the booby traps, but that was all right, as long as it promoted a good spirit among them.

One of the warriors brought Bird's horse to her and she told Gabe and Ezra, "Come with us, we have a lodge ready for you." Ezra looked at Gabe, smiling, and the two swung back aboard and followed the girl. The warriors followed behind, prompting both Gabe and Ezra to look back often, feeling a little uncomfortable with the dog soldiers, all of whom looked fierce and intimidating, behind them.

They left the narrow valley, rode over a long finger of dry land that pointed into a larger valley, and once crested, saw a much wider and greener valley that sidled up to a steep slope that lay like an orange curtain hanging from the rim rock that marked the top of a long mesa which seemed to stand guard over the green valley. Nestled in the bottom was the village, with what Gabe guessed to be near a hundred tipis, and innumerable people scattered among them. Downstream in the distance an expansive horse herd grazed, but what amazed Gabe was the numerous garden patches that lay on the slight slope above the village. Even from the distance, he recognized squash, corn and more. It was easy to make out the extensive irrigation system that came from a carved-out ditch that stole water from the feeder creeks that trailed off into the stream at the bottom of the wide canyon, a stream that was straddled by the village.

As they neared, they were confronted by a barrier of mounted warriors that stood ready for any attack by their enemy, the Apsáalooke. The warrior who spoke to Bird rode ahead and gave the report which was quickly relayed along the line and shouts and war cries filled the air. Many of the warriors rode back into the village, spreading the news and people came from the tipis and quickly resumed their lives. Children wasted no time resuming their hoop games and more. Women returned to cook pots and fires, others to hide scraping and sewing and other mundane but welcome duties. By the time Gabe and company entered the village, they were greeted over and over again with smiles, waves, and shouted greetings. Bird led the visitors toward the center of the village and stopped before a large hide lodge beside which sat several older men, seated on blankets and looking up at the visitors.

Bird spoke softly and told them to get down to meet the elders. Gabe glanced at Ezra, nodded, and both men stepped down, holding one rein of their horses as they stood before the elders. It was a familiar scene, one they had experienced among the Osage, Pawnee, Omaha and more. Bird stepped forward, head and eyes down and spoke to the men, motioning back to Gabe and Ezra as she continued to address the men. She turned to them and said, "Do you know the Spanish language?"

"Yes, I do," answered Gabe.

"Then my mother's sister, Nanawu, Little Striped Squirrel, will translate for the elders, if you speak in Spanish," explained Bird.

An older woman, grey haired and wrinkled, but steady on her feet, came from the group beside the tipi and stepped beside Gabe, facing the elders. Bird spoke in Shoshoni to introduce the men, referring to Gabe as Claw of the Bear and Ezra as Black Buffalo. She nodded to Nanawu to introduce the elders.

"This is Crooked Leg, son of Weasel Lungs," began the older woman as she nodded to the man on the left of the group of four. "He is Three Horns, this man is Buffalo Tail, and this man is Twists His Tail." At each introduction, the man referenced gave a slight nod but did not change his stoic expression. Crooked Leg leaned forward slightly and motioned for the two to sit on the blankets provided opposite the elders.

Both Gabe and Ezra sat, cross-legged, and facing the men and waited for them to speak. Crooked Leg looked from one elder to the others and then to the visitors, then began. "You have brought two of our young people back. We are grateful." The old woman had remained standing and looked to the visitors and translated.

Gabe grinned, "We have learned much from your young people. They have helped us as well."

"Uhn," grunted Crooked Leg, who Gabe took to be the chief.

"Singing Bird said the Apsáalooke leader was Hó-ra-tó-a

and he left because his medicine was bad. What was done to make him think his medicine was bad?"

Gabe chuckled and began to explain about the many booby traps and how Singing Bird and Badger Tail had worked hard to make the traps, especially the part about the snakes. He described, with some elaboration and exaggeration, what happened when the Crow came among them and the antics of both horses and men, eliciting much laughter from the elders. He finished by explaining about the skull and the whistling arrow and the rapid gunfire, both bringing frowns that showed lack of understanding, but Gabe continued and told of the parley with the war leader and of his leaving to find his warriors. When he finished, the elders were smiling and relaxed, and the chief said, "It is good what you have done. It takes much courage to face an enemy and send him on his way without killing. It is much like what we call taking coups." Gabe and Ezra both nodded, familiar with the practice of taking coup on the enemy.

"We have prepared a lodge for you to stay with us. You are welcome to stay as long as you like," said the chief, obviously awaiting an answer.

"We are honored. We will stay, but only a short while. We want to go to the mountains and find a place to spend the winter, but we will enjoy our stay with you, and we are grateful."

"Singing Bird will show you to your lodge and Badger Tail will take care of your horses," explained Crooked Leg, waving for the young people to step forward. At Bird's nudge, both Gabe and Ezra rose, nodded to the chief and elders, and left with Bird. She spoke as she walked, "Gourd Rattler will cook for you. She is a good woman who is alone since her man was killed by the Blackfoot. If you need anything, she will get it for you." She pointed to a lodge with the entry flap thrown back, "Your things are in there and Badger Tail waits for your horses." She stood beside the entry and asked, "Will you stay with us long?"

"No, just a day or two, I reckon. We're wantin' to get to the mountains and find us a place to build a cabin or somethin' 'fore winter comes," answered Gabe.

"Our village will move back to the trees below the big mountains before the colors come."

"You mean, when the trees change colors?" asked Gabe.

"Yes. The aspen turn gold before they lose their leaves. That is the time we will move back to our winter camp. This place," using a wide sweep of her hand to indicate the valley, "has no water in the winter. The wind is bad and the snow drifts very deep. We go higher into the trees, near a lake where there is water all winter."

"Then maybe we can visit, once everybody is moved in for the winter."

"I would like that," answered Bird with a coy smile.

26 / Mountains

It was another of those heart-tugging goodbyes. The men had become attached to the youngsters, both learning from them and teaching, and as Gabe put it, "It's kinda like sayin' goodbye to your own kids!"

"Ummhmmm, but at least we know they're gonna be fine cuz they're with their people," observed Ezra as he turned in his saddle for one last glimpse of the people of the Kuccuntikka village of the Shoshoni. Singing Bird and Badger Tail had ridden with them a short distance to say their goodbyes, and now were headed back to the village as they too turned to wave goodbye to their friends and rescuers.

"Crooked Leg talked about a valley he called the Wuhnzee Gahdtuhd, Nanawu said that meant Pronghorn Sitting. But he also said there was a river that came from the mountains called Wuhnzee Ohgway, Pronghorn River, and if we followed it upstream into the mountains, we'd find some places to build a cabin, but he also said there were some caves we might like," remarked Gabe.

"I ain't too fond of caves, but then again, buildin' a cabin seems like a lot of work," replied Ezra.

"Mebbe, but when you do, then you've got somethin' to call home."

Ezra nodded to the northwest, "That's what I want to call home!"

They had broken from the valley, following a trail that took them to the crest of a rimrock lined plateau and now sat staring at the long line of Wind River Mountains. The distant granite tipped peaks were devoid of timber, but still held glaciers that gleamed white in the crevices and crevasses that scarred the mountains. But the mighty mountains seemed to Gabe to be the very pillars of Heaven, supporting the vast expanse of blue that canopied overhead, totally free of any clouds, bright sunshine spotlighting the mountains that the men had sought to see for so long.

Ezra, standing in his stirrups, relaxed and dropped into his saddle, smiling as he looked at Gabe, "They are somethin' ain't they?"

"Everything we dreamed about! And more!"

"And lookee yonder," started Ezra as he pointed to the mountain range, "That white stuff, is that snow?"

"Probably glacier ice, but maybe snow."

"But it's summertime!"

"Not up there! From what I know about the Alps, there's places high up that the snow never melts, just adds layers to the glaciers, and the Rockies are no different. And it's not unusual to get a snowstorm in the middle of summer!"

"Now, that's a bit hard to believe. But," he nodded toward the mountains, "I guess that's proof."

Gabe stood in his stirrups, looking to the foothills that stretched to the north, then pointing, he said, "That second cut there, looks like that might be the canyon that Crooked Leg mentioned." The broad shoulders of the mountains were cut by deep ravines that held the runoff creeks and rivers that shed the snowmelt in the spring and the cloudbursts in the summer with a few deeper cuts that told of canyons that had been carved by eons of runoff. The lower end of the shouldered foothills appeared barren of the black timber that marked the upper reaches and trailed off to the flats that held a wide expanse of the green valley, Wuhnzee Gahdtuhd.

With another long look at the mountains that marched off to the north, they gigged their horses to a trot as they pointed toward the foothills. They were just beginning to understand the difference in the high mountain air of the west and what they were used to in the east. Distances were hard to determine, the clear air making distant things seem closer. What they had expected to be a couple hours ride, took the rest of the day before they found themselves at the mouth of the canyon of the Wuhnzee Ohgway, or Pronghorn River. He had also learned the Crow called this the Popo Agie, or Gurgling River.

With a quick stop at the river, they refreshed themselves and the horses, and with a last glimpse of the sun as it dropped behind the mountains, barely seen through the notch of the canyon walls, they moved into the mouth of the canyon staying on the north bank of the river. Thick willows and alders hugged the river, forcing the riders to the foot of the hills as they pushed into the canyon. With a steep timber covered slope on their left, the granite cliffs on their right, they felt crowded between them. Lined out in single file, Gabe trailing the sorrel pack-laden mare, Ezra leading the loaded mustangs, the hooves clattering on the rocks echoed and bounced through the gorge. Gabe reined up, stood in his stirrups to survey the canyon ahead, then twisted around, "Let's go back to the mouth of that little valley across the stream. That looks better than anything I can see ahead."

Ezra reined his bay around, the mustangs tugging at the lead line, and pushed through the thin willows to cross the narrow river to take the trail on the opposite bank. The place chosen by Gabe was less than fifty yards downstream and once clear of the steep slopes, the valley opened into a nice grassy flat with scattered juniper that hugged some rocky cliffs. Ezra smiled as he surveyed the area, picked a spot near the trees and reined up to look back at Gabe. With a wave of his hand and a nod from Gabe, Ezra stepped down and started stripping the gear from the horses. It had been a long day's travel and both man and beast would enjoy the rest.

They made their camp on the lee side of the cliffs, but close enough to take advantage of the sheltering overhang. There were signs of other camps, none recent, and Gabe looked about for any sign of who might have been here before them. But the only evidence was from early campfires, nothing more. While Ezra sat on an upturned log, Gabe leaned back against his saddle and with one hand behind his head, the other holding the coffee cup, he breathed deep, grinned, "Even the air is better here! Don'tcha think?"

Ezra chuckled, "It's just air, Gabe. Might smell a little more like pine, but it's just air."

Gabe looked at Ezra with a furrowed brow, "No imagination, that's your problem, no imagination. Here we are at the base of the mountains we talked and dreamed about for years, and you just ain't appreciatin' it!"

"I'll appreciate it better with a full stomach and a night's rest," declared Ezra, adjusting the willows that held their venison steaks over the fire.

"Why am I not surprised at that?"

Dusk had dropped its curtain and shortly thereafter, both men were in their bedrolls. The clear night held a myriad of stars almost within reach as both men lay with hands behind their heads, staring at the night sky. Gabe broke the silence, "They look so close it's as if we could reach up and touch 'em."

"And there's so many! I ain't never seen a night sky like that. Even the Milky Way seems to be hanging right over that hilltop yonder."

"No wonder the natives regard it as the road to the other side, or what some would say is the path to heaven. And that big three-quarter moon looks like it's restin' on the mountain top."

Ezra added, *"'The heavens declare the glory of God; and the firmament sheweth His handiwork.'* But I never imagined I'd ever be layin' here under such beauty as that."

A contemplative silence settled over the camp as the men drifted off to sleep to the lullaby of the chuckling river below while the horses stood three legged at the picket line. The animals were secluded between the cliff face and the sleeping men, but Ebony, as always was nearest Gabe. And it was the big black that awakened Gabe with his snorting and pawing. When Gabe looked through sleep filled eyes, he was brought fully awake at the sight of the big eyes and flared nostrils of the black. His ears were forward, and he was looking toward the river below. Gabe snatched up his rifle as he came from his blankets and searched the shadows by the river. The blue light from the moon gave just enough illumination to see, but the shadows from the thick willows and scattered aspen and alders prevented recognition of whatever had disturbed the stallion.

Gabe stepped back closer to the horses, stroking the neck of Ebony and speaking softly to reassure all the animals. He glanced at the others, noticed the mustangs were also watching below. Something had spooked all of them and the mustangs were more familiar with the wilderness than the others. Gabe paid close attention to their action. Both were showing nervousness, tugging at their tethers, keeping their eyes on the brush by the river. Gabe looked again, heard Ezra speak, "Can you make out anything?"

"No, but there's somethin' down there that's got 'em

spooked."

Gabe took a step forward when he heard a rhythmic grunting and huffing, then a splashing of the water that told of something crossing the river, and it was in a hurry. Then a thunderous roar split the night, reverberating between canyon walls, and followed by another and another. Gabe and Ezra looked at one another and quickly turned back toward the river, yet casting their eyes side to side, searching for cover or a shooting position. Gabe said, "That sounds like more'n one! You don't suppose their fightin', do ya?"

"Could be, but whatever's goin' on, they sound almighty big!"

The men stood almost shoulder to shoulder, both holding their rifles across their chest, unconsciously manipulating their fingers to feel the triggers and hammer of their rifles for reassurance. With a quick glance down to reassure himself that the frizzen was seated, Gabe lifted his eyes again to the brush at the river. Massive shadows were thrashing about in the brush, but all the men could see was dark forms. The repeated roars and snapping of jaws told them the combatants were bears, but nothing more. The men stepped side to side, trying for a better look, but neither dared to be so foolish as to go nearer the fight. After just a few moments, although it seemed more like an hour, the noise abated, and with only a few grunts, the battle was over.

Gabe looked back at Ebony and the mustangs, and all seemed to be settling down, but the stallion kept his head up and watching the brushy bank by the river. Gabe stroked his neck and head, speaking softly to the big stallion and finally he lowered his head, bending his neck to turn and rub his muzzle against Gabe's side.

"I don't know if I can go back to sleep after that. I shore don't want one o' them things to come up here sniffin' around for dessert!" drawled Ezra, setting his Lancaster rifle butt down and holding it close to his side.

"Then why don't you stoke up the fire a mite and heat up the coffee?" suggested Gabe as he walked to the log beside the fire.

27 / Discovery

Gabe sat atop the long ridge above the camp, Bible in his lap as he watched the sun chin itself on the ridge that paralleled the one where he sat. He had watched the first sign of the rising sun as it painted the bottoms of the three long narrow clouds that lay above the horizon and enjoyed his time with his Lord in prayer as the golden orb slowly showed itself. Now it bent long rays to search valley bottoms and begin the new day. He turned to look over his left shoulder, looking at the valley of the Popo Agie and the stream's course in the bottom of the canyon. He looked beyond at the point of the shoulder of the ridge and searched for sign of the combat that took place in the darkness. The ground at stream's edge was torn up as if a novice farmer and his plow pulling mule had an interminable argument and only the plow won. He chuckled to himself and thought, *If I only had some seeds, maybe I could plant a garden!*

He rose to return to camp, knowing Ezra was probably

already returning from his time with the Lord. They had gone in opposite directions, each seeking a solitary place that afforded a view of the day's beginning. While Gabe climbed the ridge west of their camp, Ezra scaled the steeper slope to the east. From the time Gabe listened to Ezra about his need of coming to know the Lord as Savior and he responded by accepting that gift of eternal life, the two friends had consistently spent the waking moments of each day with the Lord in prayer and Bible reading.

Ezra was the first to return and was busy stoking up the fire for their morning fare and Gabe said, "Since you've got things underway, I'm gonna go take a look at the battle ground from last night!"

"Take your rifle! The horses still aren't comfortable with things. They're probably still smellin' bear."

The soil was churned and turned, grass clods thrown about, willows ripped up, and the smell of bear was everywhere. Gabe walked with careful steps, looking at the sign of a major battle between the beasts of the mountains. He had never seen a grizzly bear close-up but had heard many stories about them from both Indians and men of the mountains. They were said to be nine to ten feet tall when standing, and to have paws the size of a man's head and claws longer than a man's fingers.

As he looked around, he knew whatever had made this mess had to have been massive and powerful. The thought of two beasts like that fighting so near brought a rush of adrenaline that tensed him and alerted his senses and more so with every step upon the scene of the conflict. Then something caught his eye beneath the bent-over willows, and he drew close. It was a patch of brown fur, and when he lifted the branches, he saw the carcass of a Grizzly cub, but even the cub was large. Probably a yearling, thought Gabe. He knew that a big boar would often kill the cub of a sow, making her come into season sooner so he could breed with her. But this boar had met a mad mama and she had given him a battle he would long remember, if he survived. He had seen several splotches of blood and knew one or both of the combatants were injured, perhaps badly.

He took another look around, found the tracks where the bears had taken separate paths away from the creek bottom, but both were headed upstream, where the men planned to go in search of their new homesite. He shook his head, turned away from the tracks, and started back to camp. As they ate, Gabe explained his findings and added, "We're gonna have to keep a sharp eye out. They headed upstream, exactly where we're headed today."

"Well I'll tell you right now, I ain't spendin' no winter hibernatin' with bears!" answered Ezra, finishing his morning brew. He had found some chicory and sliced the roots thin, dried and roasted it, and ground it together with the coffee to make the coffee last longer. It was different but satisfying. He looked up at Gabe, "How ya like the coffee?"

Gabe chuckled, "You mean the chicory?"

Ezra laughed, "Just tryin' to stretch it out a mite. At the

rate we're goin' I figger we'll be plumb outta coffee 'bout Christmas time!"

"Well, it tastes a little different, but since it's all we got, it's fine."

The rising sun was painting the east face of the ridge with a golden glow when the men rode away from their night's camp. They chose not to make it a base camp, concerned about the return of the bears, and trailed the packhorses as they rounded the shoulder of the ridge and pointed up the valley. With the river, if it could be called that since it averaged about twenty-five feet wide and about two feet deep, hugging the shoulder, they were forced to cross over. But after about a half-mile, they had to cross again as the river twisted its way through the canyon floor. They had crossed the second time when Gabe reined back to the creek's edge, stood in his stirrups and pushed his hat back, shaking his head.

"What?" asked Ezra as he pulled alongside.

"Either that's the biggest spring I ever saw, or . . ." started Gabe, pointing to a wide still pool that appeared to be the sole source of water for the river.

Ezra scowled, stepped down and walked to the edge of the bluff that overlooked the pool, "I dunno, but one thing's for sure, there's some mighty nice trout down there!" pointing to the water below.

Gabe stepped down and walked closer, looking where Ezra pointed and saw so many big trout in the pool that measured about fifty by a hundred feet and so deep they couldn't see the bottom, that the water churned with their movement. He guessed the fish to average twenty-four to thirty inches and at least two pounds each. "Almost makes me hungry for trout!"

"It would be a nice change, but I reckon we'll see other pools or streams where we can get some. If we tried to go down there and get some o' them, we'd prob'ly fall in and become fish food!"

"You're probably right about that, 'sides, we got to find us a place for the winter."

They turned back to the horses and mounted up, as Ezra asked, "How d'ya s'pose that spring or whatever it is, is so big?"

"Dunno, but it's just one o' the wonders we'll see in these mountains, I imagine."

They had ridden about a half-mile when Gabe reined up again, sat in his saddle, hands on the pommel as he shook his head in wonder. He nodded down a slight embankment as Ezra came near and the men watched as another river, or perhaps the same one, pushed up against a rock wall and disappeared. They looked at the stream coming from up the canyon, and then where it crashed against the rock wall and Ezra said, "Guess that answers my question. Must go underground and come back up down yonder."

"Prob'ly. Sure makes you wonder though, don't it?" asked Gabe as he reined Ebony back to the trail that hugged the bottom of the steep sloping canyon wall on their right. The canyon walls seemed to push close in, narrowing the steep defile, but the trail held to the shoulder of the south facing slope, often rising above the valley floor where the creek chuckled past. Gabe guessed they had come about three or four miles when the stream bent around a talus slope that pushed into the canyon bottom. They stayed on the narrowing trail, occasionally with the right stirrup touching the canyon wall while the left stirrup hung above empty space.

They rounded the talus slope, and the shoulder of the granite topped mountains held the trail secure above the stream that now crashed down the rocky bottom, showing nothing but white water as the tumbling falls offered a symphony of sound that echoed across the canyon. A short distance further, and the trail and stream parted company at the insistence of a granite mound that rose streamside and offered no shoulder for a trail. The men had just a glimpse of waterfalls that tumbled down the mountain side between the granite knob and steep walled cliffs opposite.

The trail switched back on itself three times before cresting on the saddle between the granite knob and the taller timber covered mountain to the north. Once over the saddle, a long basin filled with aspen invited them onward. At the upper end and bottleneck of the basin, the trail overlooked the stream that had split as it cascaded down the steep rocks, tumbling in several falls, splashing white water on its path. Both men looked in wonder at the sight, framed between granite knolls with a background of the Wind River Mountain range. They sat for a moment, drinking in the splendor, then turned away to follow the trail even higher.

One aspen basin opened to another and they climbed higher with every step. To his right, Gabe spotted a steep talus slope that faced the east, yet with chokecherry and service berry bushes clustered at its base. A small stream, shallow and clear, trickled from beyond the brush and wound its way to the bottom of the basin, to disappear among the aspen. He nodded to Ezra and pointed, then reined Ebony toward the sight. There was something that attracted him, maybe the split in the talus or the brush but he had to take a closer look. Once there, he stepped down and walked among the bushes, and as he suspected, the bank of berry bushes had obscured a wide overhang of the cliff face that had pushed the fallen stone to either side, and offered shelter to anyone or anything that found the opening. He called back to Ezra, "Come take a look!"

Ezra stepped down from his bay, tied it off to a big branch of the brush, and pushed his way through. The men stood before an overhang that extended back into the face of the granite monolith at least thirty to forty feet. With the face about fifty feet across, it offered ample space for them and their horses, and a dark recess teased with even more space. Gabe walked forward, kicked at some charcoal tipped sticks and said, "Somebody's camped here before, but looks like a mighty long time ago."

Ezra had turned around, looking over the brush, pushed some aside, and gazed at the vista below. He turned back around, guessed the height of the opening to be about ten to twelve feet at the apex sloping to four to five feet at the ends. "We could even close it off with upright timbers," he suggested, looking at Gabe.

"Yeah, I bet we could, and with only one wall to build, it'd go up faster'n a cabin."

Ezra chuckled, "That's what I'm thinkin'." He grinned at his friend and they knew they had found their winter home.

28 / Preparations

For the first time since they left Pennsylvania, the men unpacked the tools they purchased in Pittsburgh, just before boarding the flatboat to go down the Ohio river. Gabe's prized tool was the Sheffield Saw, but the double-bladed axe would be even more useful. They chose to cut the needed timber well away from the building site and make random cuts so as not to give away their location. Ponderosa pine, spruce and fir were abundant on the higher reaches of the mountain slopes and they began working together, using all the horses to snake the trees from the woods and back to the site. Each trip, they tried to take a slightly different route, preferring to leave no trail behind them.

At the end of the first week, they had a pile of logs they thought would be suitable for the task, and they picketed the horses in the tall grass of an upper meadow and returned to set about trimming and shaping the logs. They enjoyed the work, though every day brought sore muscles and tired bodies and the ice-cold waters of the creek were less than inviting and used as sparingly as possible.

By the end of the second week, they stood back and looked at the finished wall, the double-door entry, and the shuttered windows, and smiled at one another. Gabe said, "Looks like home to me!"

"Yeah, but it's an empty home. Now we need to make us some furniture, like a couple beds, a table, some chairs, and maybe even make us a fireplace below that chimney vent we found in the corner yonder."

"And we need some sort of corral or wall to separate the stable from the cabin portion. No rest for the weary!" declared Gabe as he pulled open the door. They did their best to keep from destroying the berry bushes, both to keep them for the fruit but also as cover for their cabin. The less obvious it was, the better. There was no benefit in flaunting their presence, and once the aspen shed their leaves, there would be nothing but the berry bushes to camouflage their existence.

The next week was spent in the furniture making, but they took a few breaks to explore their new home. The dark maw at the back beckoned and with sap covered pine torches in hand, they started to explore. The floor at the back of the cavern rose suddenly, then dropped off in the darkness. They held torches high and crawled over the rise and were surprised when they entered a massive cathedral like cavern. Stalagmites of various colors marched up and down and stalactites hung like giant icicles reaching down to meet the marching forms below. Gabe spoke, "Well, would you look at that!" and his words bounced around the cavernous room.

Every move of their torches made shadows dance on the walls, and light glisten on the moist formations. Gabe looked at the flame of his torch, saw it flutter, and looked toward the far wall of the cave, "There's air coming from there. We might have a back way outta here!" They started across the cavern floor, gauging the size of the larger grotto to be about a hundred feet by a hundred fifty. The formations hugged the walls and the central area had a ceiling at least thirty feet high. The water trickled along the side wall and pushed its way past the floor rise to exit the entry under their log wall. High up a wide crevice showed a ragged opening that allowed dim sunlight to show through.

When they neared the rear of the cavern, a break in the formations showed a narrow declivity that split the calcium pillars and the fresh air in his face gave Gabe direction. The passageway widened and within moments, sunlight showed. The opening was obscured by thick brush, mostly mountain mahogany, but it was easy to see through the maze and know this would be their needed exit. They would have to widen the walkway to the rear opening, make it wide enough to lead horses through, but little else would be needed. "We'll need to scout out the cover on the outside, both the entry and that split in the rocks high up. If we're gonna have a cookfire, the smoke needs to get out, but it also needs to be filtered with brush and trees and such," suggested Gabe.

"I'll let you tend to that. I've got some more work to do on our furniture. Then I want to get started on the fireplace," replied Ezra. He had always enjoyed working with his hands to create things and often toiled with his father crafting woodwork. It had been a lifelong hobby of his father who said, "It frees up my mind. You know, clears out the cobwebs and lets me think clearly. What with all the problems of people in the church, I need that every now and then." Ezra just enjoyed the creating of things that might outlast him.

While Ezra enjoyed his work inside, Gabe tended to things outside. The crevice in the roof of the cavern was well protected by a stack of flat slide rock and some ground hugging juniper. The back entry was also hidden behind a sizable cluster of cedar and mountain mahogany that made the opening almost impossible to see from the trees.

During the day, they would take the horses to different mountain meadows to graze but always bring them back to the cave at night. Gabe would usually gather several bunches of grass, bind them up and pack them back for the winter store for the horses. He also spent most early mornings and evenings meat hunting and the large cavern had become a cooling room for the fresh meat. He built several racks to hang the quarters of meat, letting them develop that hard crust of protection as they cooled.

By the end of the third week, the work was done on both the interior and exterior of their winter abode and they applied themselves with renewed interest in hunting and preparing their winter stores. They smoked elk and deer strips and after several days of feasting on fresh trout, they began smoking the fish. Ezra was better at finding the variety of plants, roots, and such that could be dried and kept for later use, and he enjoyed his solitary times in the woods.

Gabe usually climbed the granite knoll behind the cabin for his morning time with the Lord, but this morning he chose to climb higher to a shoulder of the tall mountain that loomed to the north. He wanted an unobstructed view of the rising sun and knew the shoulder offered just such a promontory. He zig-zagged his way up the steep slope, guided by the dim pre-dawn light. He picked his way among long dead fire-blackened trees that made his climb more of an obstacle course, but he soon topped out on the bald knob of the mountain's shoulder. As he sat down on a flat granite slab, he looked to his left and noticed a faint game trail that came from the bottom and cut through a notch to round the mountain-top to disappear into the black timber beyond. "Hmmm, that's a trail I'll need to remember," he whispered to himself as he looked back to the east.

He enjoyed his quiet moments of reflection and communing with God. It was a special treat to watch the slow rising sun as it colored the eastern sky, sending shafts of hues of gold and pink across the broad canopy to reflect on the world below. When the golden orb peeked over the ragged horizon, the brightness shone on and warmed his face as he sat, eyes closed, absorbing the morning warmth. He lowered his chin to his chest, looked at the Bible in his lap and began to read aloud, *"Let the words of my mouth, and the meditation of my heart, be acceptable in thy sight,*

O Lord, my strength and my redeemer." Then a breath of wind flipped several pages of the Bible before Gabe dropped his hand upon it to stop the fluttering and read where his finger pointed, *"He healeth the broken in heart, and bindeth up their wounds. He telleth the number of the stars; he calleth them all by their names. Great is our Lord, and of great power: his understanding is infinite."*

He paused, thinking about the words and lifted his eyes to the morning sun and smiled. Then from behind him, a familiar voice said, "Is that true?"

Gabe spun around to look behind him and shook his head, "Why do you always do that?" he asked as he grinned at Singing Bird, standing with hands clasped before her and a smile tugging at the corners of her mouth.

She giggled as she ducked her head and came closer. "It is so easy, you are so . . . intent on what you do when you pray."

"What are you doing here?" asked Gabe, looking around to see if there were any others with her, but only a lone horse stood tethered nearby.

"It is the sickness. There were others that did not become sick until they returned to the village, now many are sick, and we left to get away before we took the plague of death." Tears welled in her eyes and chased one another down her cheeks as she dropped her head. Gabe motioned her to sit beside him and once seated, she lay her head on his shoulder as he comforted her with his arm around her shoulders.

"How many are there with you?"

"This many," she held up both hands, all fingers extended,

and flashed them twice.

"Where?"

She turned and pointed beyond the talus of granite to the valley of the Popo Agie, "There. Crooked Leg said you would be near, and I said you knew about the sickness. Those that are with me are not sick, but . . ."

"Let's go down to our cabin. Ezra will be glad to see you."

"I saw him. He told me where you would be," she answered, showing a quick smile.

Gabe stood and with an arm around her shoulders, started back to the cabin. He thought to himself, *How quickly things change. I thought we were about ready for winter, now . . .*

29 / Neighbors

"Is it?" asked Singing Bird, walking beside Gabe. The two were making their way down from the north mountain to their abode in the granite knoll.

"Is it what?" replied Gabe, slightly confounded. His mind had been swirling with thoughts and questions about the Shoshoni and the smallpox disease. *How many were infected? What would they need to do to stop the progress of the disease? Could it be stopped? Apparently, Bird and her brother had developed an immunity but what about the others?*

"Is it true? What you were saying when I asked you up there?" nodding back toward the mountain promontory.

"Oh, yes it's true. I was reading from the Bible," he held it out for her to see, "and it is always true. It tells us about God and how we should live."

"You said He heals the broken. My people are broken with the white man's sickness. Can your God fix that?" she asked with both doubt and sincerity, hopeful of a positive answer to their dilemma.

"What I read said, *'He healeth the broken in heart, and bindeth up their wounds.'* And He can do all that, but it starts with our relationship with Him." He stopped and looked directly at Bird, "God deals with the eternal, or those things that are more important than just what we go through here on this earth, although all that we do is important to him. He wants us to have a place in Heaven with Him, a home for all eternity."

"That is something I have wanted to know for as long as I can remember. My people also call Him, Our Father. But we believe that after we die we make a long journey to the land beyond the sun," she pointed to the west, "and sometimes we come back as another being, like an elk, or deer, or bear, or something else. Is that what you believe?"

Gabe smiled and answered, "No. We believe that when we die, if we know the Lord as our Savior, we will spend all of eternity in a place called Heaven." He pointed to the canopy of blue, "and that place is beyond the sky. That's where we will live with God and others that have gone before us, for all time."

"But you say we have to know the Lord . . ." she frowned, "What does that mean?"

He pointed to a flat boulder by the trail and motioned for them to sit. He turned to her, "Just like with you and me. We did not know one another until that day we met on the trail. As we came to know one another, we became friends and then we learned to trust one another, because we believe each other. And with God, it's like that also. First, we know Him, then we believe Him, and then we trust Him to take us to Heaven when we die. All along, we learn more and trust more and learn to love more."

"Can I do that? Get to know Him and trust Him?"

"Of course. The Bible," he held it up again, "tells us how. See there's four things we need to know. First, is that we are all sinners, *(Romans 3:23)* or that we have done wrong, like mistreating others, or not telling the truth. You understand that?"

"Yes. I have done wrong things before," she looked up at Gabe and hurriedly added, "but I try to do better each time!"

Gabe smiled and continued, "Well, because we're sinners, having done wrong, the penalty or punishment, is death. *(Romans 6:23a)* That's not just dying, that's spending all our days after we die in a terrible place called Hell. Do you understand that?"

"I think so. But I don't want to spend days in a place like that."

"Good. You don't have to, and God doesn't want us to. That's why He sent His Son to pay the price for our sin by dying on the cross for us. Because He did that, we don't have to pay that penalty or punishment because He did it for us. *(Romans 5:8)"* He looked at her to see if she understood and smiled as she nodded but waited for the next thing.

"And because we're sinners, and the penalty is death, a penalty that Christ paid for us, then all we have to do is to accept that truth. Now, because He did that, He also purchased for us a free gift and that gift is eternal life *(Romans 6:23b),* or a life for eternity in Heaven with Him."

Singing Bird smiled, hugged her knees to her chest and said, "Oh! I want that! I want that gift so I can live in Heaven!"

Gabe smiled and added, "Then all you need to do is *Confess with thy mouth the Lord Jesus, and shalt believe in thine heart that God hath raised Him from the dead, thou shalt be saved. (Romans 10:9-10) For whosoever shall call upon the name of the Lord shall be saved. (Romans 10:13)* That just means that if you believe with all your heart, you can pray and ask God for that free gift of eternal life, and He will give it to you. Do you understand that?"

"Yes, but how do I pray and ask?"

"Simple. I'll lead us in prayer and help you, but it's just a simple asking." Gabe took her hand and bowed his head and began to pray a simple prayer asking God to heed the prayer of Singing Bird, then he led her as she prayed to accept Christ as her Savior. When they finished she looked up at Gabe, smiling, and jumped off the rock and said, "We must tell Ezra!" and took his hand in hers and quickly walked the rest of the way, her horse trailing behind them, to the cabin.

Ezra was waiting by the doorway when they came down from the mountain. He leaned against the log frame and with arms crossed, he grinned, "I see she found you!"

Gabe chuckled, "And I'm not all she found!" He looked at Bird and added, "Tell him."

The girl, smiling broadly, looked at Ezra and said, "I

prayed to your God and asked for the gift to live in Heaven!"

Ezra pushed away from the cabin logs, and stepped toward her, smiling and with arms held wide. She stepped into his hug and stood on tip toes to return the hug. When they stepped back, she said, "I am so happy. Before we came here, I had wondered about what you believed, and now I know, because I believe that too!"

"Well, I reckon we all have a lot to learn, but for right now, let's go inside, have some coffee and you can tell us all about what has happened with your people."

"When our village left for the buffalo hunt, three bands went to different places. The French trader and his woman visited one band before they came to ours. They had many blankets to trade for pelts and many traded. No one was sick in the first band. But when his woman got sick when they were with our band, some of our people became sick. First, they hurt here and here," she pointed to her head and stomach, "then later they had the spots and blisters. Then many died but some had just a few spots and they lived. That's when our band started back to the village and my family and others had to stay behind when they got sick.

"Then after you left our village, others started getting sick and some thought you had brought it, but I told them you helped us and did not have the sickness. But many of our people became sick and then my mother's sister, Nanawu, thought we should leave and take those who had been with our band and did not get sick, with us. Nanawu and her son,

Chochoco, and his family also came."

"Has anyone else gotten sick since you left the village?" asked Ezra.

"No one."

"Did any others leave the village?" asked Gabe.

"Yes, but I do not know where they went. Crooked Leg told Nanawu that you would be in this place and thought we should come here."

"How long since you left the village?" asked Gabe.

"Three days," answered Bird.

Ezra looked at Gabe, "So, what do you think?"

Gabe frowned, shook his head, then answered, "Well, the incubation period of smallpox is one to two weeks, give or take, and once it breaks out it is very contagious. Maybe . . ." he thought for a moment, then continued, "Maybe if we kind of separate the families and others, kept them apart for ten to fifteen days, then if any break out, each group can be treated separately and even isolate the infected ones. If no one comes down, then they'll be alright, but if . . ." and he shrugged his shoulders, having no answer for the 'if.'"

"Then I suggest we go on down to their camp 'fore they get their lodges all set up and tell 'em what they need to do," suggested Ezra. He received a nod from both Gabe and Bird and the three rose to do as decided.

30 / Measures

"Singing Bird said some that were with her band had the sickness but are now well. Are there any here?" asked Gabe. He waited while Nanawu translated for him. He and Ezra had spoken with the leader of the band, Broken Lance, and told him what to expect. The leader then asked Gabe to tell the people and Gabe stood before them to prepare them. He watched as Nanawu translated and saw one woman and a young man, standing beside one another, step forward. He looked at them and asked, "You had the spots and now are well?"

Both nodded and the woman pointed to fresh scars on her arms that told the story.

"Good. You cannot get the sickness again, but you can help any that do. Will you do that?" he asked. He watched as they listened to Nanawu. They looked at one another and slowly nodded their heads, howbeit reluctantly and fearfully.

"I promise you, you cannot get the sickness again," he

reassured them. Then turning to the rest, he began to explain about isolating themselves from one another, but only for three hands of days. He explained about the symptoms of headache, fever, stomachache, and more, then how they should respond if one of their group got sick. There was some mumbling about separating, but they agreed and once Gabe finished, they parted and began to set up their camp as he had instructed.

Most natives were diligent about hygiene, but Gabe had cautioned them to be extra careful. There should be no touching of one another, bathing should be done downstream and never together and wait until after the current had taken the water away. Horses were always kept downstream of the camp and even the horses were not to be handled any more than necessary. Clothing, blankets, robes, were not to be shared or handled by anyone else. The utmost care was encouraged and most abided by the directions. All had seen how terrible and deadly the disease was and none wanted to experience it, so even though it was against their usual way, they agreed to adhere to the guidance for the three hands, or fifteen, days.

It is not the nature of the native to complain or vocalize minor pains or inconveniences, so it was no surprise to Gabe to learn that one of the women had been experiencing the symptoms of fever and stomachache. It was early on the second day that he, accompanied by Nanawu and the Shaman, Big Crow, started for the lodge of the woman. But before they neared, they heard a loud wail come from within, and the daughter of the woman throw back the entry hide and step from the lodge, a frightened look on her face. The three trotted up to the lodge and Gabe asked, "Your mother?"

"Yes. She has the spots! My father is with her," answered the girl known as Little Basket.

Gabe said, "Stay here. Don't touch anything!" and motioned the other two into the lodge. The medicine man immediately began an incantation, but Gabe looked at the woman, seeing spots on her arms and a few on her face. Her husband held her in his arms and Gabe shook his head. He began, "Everything she has touched since yesterday must be taken out and burned." He looked to the far side of the lodge and asked the man, "Has she touched any of these?" pointing to the blankets and robes that lay as a bed.

Once Nanawu translated, he shook his head and pointed to those around her. Gabe then pointed to those near the woman, "Are those your robes?"

He nodded his head. Gabe turned to Big Crow, "These and these," pointing to the blankets near the woman and her man, "must be taken out and burned. Their clothing too. But no one is to touch them. Use sticks and poles but get them all. Those," pointing to those on the far side, "can be used after these are gone, but whatever happens here, they must be destroyed also.

Have the woman that agreed to help, the one who had the disease before, tend to her needs. She needs to have a cold compress, water to drink and broth maybe. Her husband cannot leave this lodge. The helper can get him food as needed, but he will soon be sick himself."

When they stepped outside, Gabe spoke to Little Basket, "You cannot go back in there. If you touch anything they have touched, you will get the sickness. We will bring you some fresh blankets, but you cannot go among the other people. Nanawu will see that you are provided for, but please do not touch or go near anything in the lodge."

"Can I speak to my mother?" asked the timid and frightened girl. Gabe guessed her to be about twelve, and answered, "Only from outside the lodge. Do not try to touch her or anything of hers or your father's. Can you do that?"

"Yes. Will my mother die?"

"Maybe. But we never know. Some have gotten the sickness and lived. We just have to wait and see."

The girl nodded, turned away and seated herself near the ring of rocks that held the embers from the night's cookfire. She dropped her head in her hands and wept. Gabe went to her, put his arm around her and held her close, letting her weep on his shoulder. Big Crow came near and placed his hand upon Gabe's shoulder and motioned for him to come along when the girl was ready to stand alone.

"Little Basket will be taken in by Runs With the Deer. She lost her man when the sickness first came to our village. She is helping those with the sickness," explained Big Crow.

Gabe was seated on a buffalo robe that lay before the fire circle beside Crow's tipi and nodded at Crow's comment, "That is good. She will need someone that understands." He looked at Crow and asked, "If they do not live through the sickness, what is the custom of your people about after?" he struggled with the question, knowing that some native peoples did not speak of the departed by name or even make reference to them. He had not learned of the practice of the Shoshoni and their custom of burial or other means of disposing of the bodies. His main concern was the disease and knowing that even the contaminated blankets and the bodies could pass the plague to others.

"When someone crosses over, their bodies are wrapped in blankets or hides, usually with what they have for the journey, weapons, and more, and we take them to a cave or a crevice in the rocks and cover them over. If it is a leader or chief, their horses are killed beside them so they will have a ride on the other side," explained Big Crow using sign language as he spoke.

"I see. Is it possible that can be done by those that are helping with the sick?"

"They will need help to take the body away."

The two discussed how the preparations should and could be made with a minimum of contact but when they spoke about a place, Gabe asked, "Do you have a location?"

"No, but we do not need it yet," replied the Shaman.

"I know of a place. I found it when I was hunting, and it might be just what we need. It is a cave that's about a half-mile up the valley."

Big Crow nodded, then added, "What you are doing for my people is a good thing. We are grateful."

Gabe was surprised by the remark. He had the impression that Big Crow resented his presence and his becoming involved with what was usually the exclusive domain of the Shaman. But he nodded his head, "I am honored that you allow me to help with your people. I have seen this sickness before among the white people and know how difficult it is to fight." He paused for a moment, then added, "If there is anything I do or say that is not acceptable among your people, I ask that you tell me so it can be corrected, until I learn more about your customs."

Big Crow looked at the white man, the first white man he had ever spoken with, and nodded. Although there had been French traders that visited their village before, he had never spoken with them and held most of them in contempt because of their disrespect for his people and their ways, but this man was different. He cared about the Shoshoni and he had not seen that among any other people. Crow spoke again, "We are grateful and believe your heart is good."

By the end of that week, the burial cave would be needed. Both father and mother of Little Basket died, and the people of the small village were frightened. Gabe and Ezra, with the help of Runs With the Deer, bound the bodies in blankets and together with personal items, a favorite basket and pot of the woman and the bow, arrows, lance and shield of the man, readied the two for burial. Chochoco, Has no Horses, the son of Nanawu, and his hunting partner, Crazy Wolf, were recruited to carry one of the bodies and followed Gabe and Ezra to the cave. A long pole was used to carry the bodies, one man on each end and the body hung from braided rawhide in the middle. Before entering the cave, a small group of mourners gathered nearby and started a mourning song. Big Crow explained the usual custom was for the mourners to pass by the body and take the hand of the departed for a last handclasp, but since that could not be allowed, they gathered for the mourning song. When the wailing and lamenting subsided, the four men took the bodies into the cave, covered them with loose stone and returned to the mourners. The procession was led by Big Crow as they returned to their lodges.

The remainder of the second week was one of trepidation as every waking morning the occupants of each lodge checked themselves and one another for any indications or symptoms of the pox. And even though there was one scare when a young boy showed some symptoms, they proved to be nothing more than a reaction to eating too many not quite ripe serviceberries. But no one showed any symptoms by the end of the third week and everyone began to feel relief, believing the crisis was over.

"I think we need to have a feast!" declared Nanawu, speaking to her son, Chochoco.

The man smiled at his mother, "Yes! Everyone needs to come together and celebrate," he answered. Then added, "We should honor our friends, Bear Claw and Black Buffalo."

Nanawu answered, "It is time for the Nuà Naza 'Nga, our dance for the time of colors. The aspen are beginning to show their gold. It would be good to have the dance and a feast to look forward to the time of colors." She smiled at her son, remembering his resentment of the white man and his friend. When they first arrived at their camp on the Popo Agie, Chochoco had been selected as a war leader and would lead hunting parties, but when Bear Claw had restricted everyone to the village, he begrudged the white man any authority over him and his hunters, but his mother had convinced him to listen. Now that his people had passed the critical time, he was anxious to lead the men on a hunt. It would be good to get back to their normal ways and prepare for the coming Yeba-mea, or moon of fall.

31 / Feast

Word spread quickly among the Shoshoni about the coming celebration. The dance of the Nuà Naza 'Nga, was a time of games and hilarity as the dancers mimicked the behaviors of the animals in the fall. Singing Bird came at a run to the cavern/cabin to tell her friends about the coming dance and feast. Ezra greeted her at the door as he was returning from taking the horses to one of the upper meadows. "So, what's got you in such a rush?" he asked as she stopped, bent over with hands on knees, trying to catch her breath. She stood upright and looked at Ezra, smiling, "There's going to be a dance and a feast! It's the dance of fall and it is great fun!"

"Well, that sounds mighty fine. Come inside and tell us about it!" he declared.

Gabe was seated at the table, reading from one of their few books. It was a well-worn copy of Thomas Paine's *Common Sense, the Rights of Man, and Other Essential Writings.* As Ezra and Bird entered, he looked up, closed the book and grinned at the two who were laughing together. Ezra looked at Gabe, "Bird tells me there's a dance and a feast the people are puttin' together and she thinks we need to come!" Gabe smiled, "Sounds good to me. What do we need to do?"

"Just come. We will have lots of food, and the dance will be very special. It is the dance we do in the fall, the time of colors, or the time of the Yeba-mea, the moon of the fall."

As they walked down the slope toward the village, the sun was dropping toward the granite tipped peaks off their right shoulder, the underbellies of the few clouds were catching some of the color and the drums were beginning in the village below. Gabe looked at Ezra, "Never thought I'd see this," he grinned as he watched his steps on the moss-covered rocks.

"See what?" asked Ezra, looking at Gabe, wondering but trying to determine if he really wanted to know the answer. He knew whenever Gabe got to feeling a little melancholy, he could be hard to live with, but usually he was in a good mood and he appeared to be smiling.

"This," he nodded toward the colors of the western sky, "that," as he pointed toward the village, "and that," pointing over his shoulder at their dwelling. "I know we talked a lot and dreamed a lot about coming to the mountains, and here we are, and it's more than we imagined!"

"Ain't it though," answered Ezra. He stopped atop a half-buried boulder, looking around at the mountains, the valley of the Popo Agie, and the village of the Shoshoni below. Then he looked back at the granite knoll that held their new home, and added, "I think this is exactly what we imagined, except for the Shoshoni, that is."

"Ummhmm, I never imagined us with neighbors, but they're good people."

Singing Bird saw them coming and waved to a group of women, then motioned to Gabe and Ezra to join her near the central fire. Gabe noticed several of the lodges had been moved closer, and the village was looking more like the villages he was used to seeing, instead of scattered about like they were during the quarantine time. A large fire was in the central compound and nearby was a large drum with three men seated around, beating a continuous rhythm that seemed to vibrate through their bodies. Ezra looked at the drummers, then to Gabe and grinned, cocking his head to the side and making a face that said more than words could express, but it was one of enjoyment.

Two women stood beside Singing Bird and she motioned the men near, "This," nodding to her left, "is Pale Otter," and this, "nodding to the woman on her right, "is Grey Dove. They will serve you during the feast. It is tradition that all warriors are to be served by chosen women that are not joined."

"That is fine. Thank you," answered Gabe.

"Uh, yeah, thank you," echoed Ezra. Gabe looked at his friend who stood staring at Grey Dove, the woman directly in front of him who stood with her head down and eyes to the ground. Her hands were clasped in front of her and she tried to sneak a quick glance at Ezra but saw him looking at her and she dropped her head again. She was older than Singing Bird, Gabe guessed her to be around eighteen winters. He glanced at Pale Otter and saw she was looking boldly at him, smiling. Her hair hung loosely over her shoulders, parted in the middle and held back by a narrow, beaded headband. She had large eyes that showed a hint of mischief or deviltry. She cocked her head slightly as she looked him over, but Gabe was taken by her beauty. Everything about her face seemed perfect, a straight nose with a slight turn-up, lips that were pouty, and a figure that filled out the fringed tunic in all the right places. She was pretty and the feeble grin that tugged at the corners of her mouth said she knew it. But Gabe liked a woman with confidence, and she showed that as well. Bird was watching the reaction of the men and grinned as she observed their responses.

The women led the men to their place beside Chochoco, Big Crow, and Broken Lance. It was a place of honor to be seated with the leaders of the band, small though it was, and to be seated at the right hand of Broken Lance, was a special honor. The drums continued and several individuals were dancing to the monotonous rhythm. All were arrayed in their finest apparel and Gabe noted the attention to detail of all the garments. Beads, porcupine quills, and elk's teeth were prominent on the women's dresses, while feathers, beads, quills and fringe dominated the men's leggings, vests, and even the breechcloths. As the men were seated on the blankets, the women left to fetch their wooden utensils and finish the preparations for the feast.

The women were attentive to every detail for the men, bringing them full platters of food and wooden cups full of drink. When Gabe took his first sip, he noticed Big Crow watching and when he choked on the ale, he looked at the Shaman and asked, "What is this?"

The Shaman chuckled, "It is a special drink we use when seeking a vision. It is made only by medicine men from corn, prickly pear, and locoweed."

With just the sip, he felt a little lightheaded and sat the cup down, as he shook his head to clear his mind. He turned slightly and spoke quietly to Ezra, "Watch that stuff! It's potent!"

Ezra chuckled and said, "It's a good thing I'm not thirsty, but we better at least act like we're drinkin' it. Don't wanna offend our hosts!"

They enjoyed the feast, the food being a tender meat in a gravy with Indian potatoes, turnips, and other vegetables they couldn't identify, but tasted very good. The women took the utensils, always serving and taking from behind the men. Pale Otter brought a woven willow back rest for Gabe and lay a wolf pelt over it and pulled Gabe back against it. When he smiled at the comfort, Otter returned his smile and spoke with sign, "It is my honor to make you comfortable."

When the leaders finished their meal, they sat back to enjoy the dance and at a signal from Broken Lance, the festivities began. Nanawu knelt behind and between Gabe and Ezra and began to explain the actions of the dancers. "This is called the Nuà Naza 'Nga, or dance of the fall or time of colors. It is a fun time and tells of the animals of our land. The man with the antlers is like the big bull elk, he is rounding up his harem of cows for the time of breeding." Several women were dancing with feather fans, giving coy looks at the man as they pranced about, tossing their heads, and pushing off one another. The man tossed his antlered head and mimicked the bugle of the elk with the high-pitched whistle followed by several grunts. As he moved about, he pushed the women together as the bull would with his harem. Then one of the women, broke from the circle and was followed by the others and the man and disappeared from the circle of light from the fire.

The tempo of the drums changed and several women wearing aprons of sage and hunkered over, came dancing, lifting their feet high and in time with the drums. "These are buffalo," commented Nanawu. Gabe saw that two of the aproned women were Pale Otter and Grey Dove, and he turned to Ezra, but his friend was gone. Gabe looked around, frowning, then saw three men, each with the headdress of a bull buffalo, dance into the firelight, and he recognized one of the men was Ezra. He chuckled at his friend, shook his head slightly as he watched the drama unfold of the bulls fighting one another, then turning to the cows, or women, and dancing after them. There was considerable flirting, even in the portrayal. Then, as with the depiction of the elk, they danced out of the firelight and went bellowing into the darkness.

The final chapter of the dance was the dramatization of the grizzly bear, portrayed by a single woman and man, and ended with the two curling up together as if in hibernation. That was the cue of the others to return and finish the dance with everyone participating. Several paired off, most already having partners, but those without, soon found a dance partner. Ezra was beside Grey Dove and Pale Otter danced around the circle until she came to Gabe and reached down to draw him into the dance.

Although neither man knew anything about the dance of the Shoshoni, they soon were enjoying the festivity and frivolity. As Gabe imitated the moves of Pale Otter, stubbing his toes in the dirt, bouncing to and fro, lifting his eyes to the starlit sky and then to the ground, he laughed as he moved, enjoying the time with this new friend. He watched her as she moved, every step showing grace and confidence, and when she looked with laughing eyes at him, his grin spread even wider. She was a beautiful woman and her charismatic ways were disarming. But the dance ended all too soon and both men, accompanied by the women, returned to their place beside the leaders, to bid them goodnight, but they had already departed to their lodges. Gabe looked at Pale Otter, signed to her, "Thank you for the dance and the food. We are grateful."

"It has been an honor to serve you," replied Otter as Dove looked at Ezra and nodded her agreement. Otter smiled, dropped her eyes, and asked, "Do you want us to come with you now?"

Gabe was surprised and glanced at Ezra then back at Otter, "Will you come in the morning for a meal with us?"

"If you want," replied Otter, obviously disappointed.

"That would be good. We will see you in the morning," he signed, turning away before his resolve weakened. Ezra clasped Dove's hand and turned away and followed his friend.

32 / Provisions

They were awakened to the smell of pork belly frying, corn-cakes cooking, and the ever present woodsmoke. Ezra tossed aside his blankets and stepped from his bunk, rubbing his eyes and pushing back his hair. In the far corner, both Pale Otter and Grey Dove were busy at the fire preparing the morning meal. Ezra looked at Gabe who was slowly rolling out, and both men stared at the women, chattering softly to one another, busy at their task. Otter turned, saw the men standing and staring, smiled, and turned back to Dove, continuing their preparations as if this was the usual routine of every morning. They had quietly entered the cabin and begun their work before the men awakened.

Gabe looked at Ezra, both men grinned and shook their heads and bent to slip on their moccasins and jackets to exit the cabin for their morning constitutional. Gabe was the first to return and grabbed the coffee pot off the table and went to the small rock-lined pool at the edge of the cavern wall and filled the pot with the cold spring water that came from deep in the cavern. He bent over beside Otter and with his free hand on her shoulder, placed the pot on the hearth, pushing it close to the flames. They smiled at one another and Gabe signed, "Smells good!" Otter nodded and looked back to the pan, flipping the pork belly and then used a stick to move some coals to cover the yampa roots that were baking underneath.

Ezra had joined them by the fire and was crushing some coffee beans and chicory on the broad flat stone beside the hearth, laid in for just that purpose, for their morning brew. He looked at Gabe, "Just like a family, don'tcha think?" He knew the women did not understand English and took advantage of that as he spoke.

Gabe chuckled, "Don't you think you might be rushing things a little?"

"Oh, I dunno. Couldn't hardly sleep last night thinkin' about 'em, and I noticed you were a bit restless your own self."

Gabe glanced up at his friend but chose not to respond. It was true, it had been a restless night and his mind had been filled with thoughts of Pale Otter. She had impressed him like no other, though he and Ezra had met many native women and others on their travels, but none that stirred him like Otter. He looked at his friend and knew they both were feeling a little melancholy or just lonely. They were at a time in their lives when most men and women were making plans or having thoughts of lives together and making a family.

Why should they be any different? Neither one had ties to the past that would prevent them from taking a wife and making their lives here in the wilderness. He glanced at the women, happily working before the fire and chattering to one another. *Maybe we ought to get to know each other a little better. Why, we can't even talk, not knowing each other's language and all,* he thought. And with that thought, he knelt beside Otter and began their first lesson. He touched her shoulder, put his finger on his chest and said, "Gabe, Gabe." Then he touched her and said, "Pale Otter, Pale Otter."

She frowned then slowly let a smile paint her face and pointed to Gabe, "G, g . . . Ga . . . buh." He nodded, said again, "Gabe." She tried again, "Ga . . buh. Gabe," and smiled as Gabe nodded his head with a broad smile. Then he pointed to her and said, "Pale Otter." She nodded and tried, "Pah . . .el . . . Aww. . ter." Gabe patiently nodded, said it again, and she successfully said her own name, "Pale Otter." And the lessons began with Ezra and Grey Dove copying their friends and learning each other's names.

After breakfast, they determined they should go on a hunt to add to their larder for the winter, and perhaps provide some for the village. They continued their lessons, rather enthusiastically, learning the names of so many everyday things in each other's language. They rode away from the cabin, taking to the high trail Gabe had spotted earlier, and by late morning they stopped near a lake that nestled in a basin about two miles behind their cabin. It had been a mild climb, but the horses took advantage of the water and graze and

Gabe motioned to the others to step down. He grabbed his Ferguson from the scabbard and just as he was swinging his leg over Ebony's rump, he saw movement at the upper end of the small lake. The lake was only about a half-mile from inlet to outlet, and half-that across. They had come from the trees along a flat grassy bank near the south end, and Gabe was watching movement closer to the inlet. He shoved the rifle back in the scabbard, dug the telescope from the saddle bags and searched the upper end. Three moose, a good-sized bull, a cow and a yearling bull, probably last year's calf, were wading into the shallow end, looking for fresh shoots among the undergrowth of the lake.

Gabe looked down at the others, "There's moose. A big bull, a cow and a yearling." He looked at Ezra, "I think I'll try for the bull. It'll take a bit o' doin', but it'll be some good meat for the winter!"

"So, what's your plan?" asked Ezra.

Gabe looked back at the animals, knowing the big bull was seldom threatened by any predator, being larger than all but the grizzly. He looked down at Ezra, "If I go around and over that bit of a shoulder," pointing to the tree covered rise on the east bank of the lake, "then I can work in closer to 'em under cover of the trees."

"You gonna use your bow or rifle?" asked Ezra.

"No reason not to use the rifle, and that big fella's gonna take some killin'. How 'bout all of us ride thataway," pointing to the rise, "and you can come with me. The ladies can keep the horses in check, and we'll do our best to sneak up on 'em."

It took only a few moments for the four to work through the trees to the ridge of the long shoulder that stood opposite a steep talus on the far shore. Covered with juniper, cedar, and a few ponderosa, the slope on the northwest side gave the men good cover. The women had tethered the horses in a black thicket, then crawled to the edge of a slight clearing on the crest that overlooked the lake. Gabe and Ezra, now on foot, moved stealthily through the timber, working toward the narrow inlet of the lake. Once at the tree line, Gabe motioned for Ezra to stop. They could see the moose, about three hundred yards from where they stood, in the shallows of the inlet. The big bull dropped his head underwater, came up with a mouthful of greenery and chomped on the plants like an ill-mannered backwoodsman. The cow nudged the yearling deeper into the water, then snatched a mouthful and began eating.

Gabe whispered to Ezra, "How 'bout you workin' your way around the tree line yonder," pointing across the flat mossy bog of the inlet, "and go to shoutin' and wavin' your arms to spook 'em outta the water. I can take a shot when they're clear, cuz I don't cotton to swimming in that cold lake water to retrieve that big boy's carcass."

"I hear ya. It'd take you, me, and the horses to get that one outta there." He lifted his eyes to the tree line and across the mossy flat. "Alright, give me about fifteen minutes or so." He stepped back into the thicker trees and started for the far shore. In just a short while, Gabe was surprised to see Ezra emerge from the aspen at the edge of the flat and step out and start hollering and waving his arms.

The cow moose jerked her head toward the ruckus, the bull brought his head from the water and looked, and without any hesitation, all three spun around and splashed their way through the shallow, heading for the trees. Gabe was waiting and the bull had no sooner paused for another look at the noisy creature by the aspen, than the big Ferguson Rifle roared and spat smoke and lead as it bucked against Gabe's shoulder. The impact of the bullet splattered wet fur and mud low on the chest of the bull, staggering him about a half step, but the bull bellowed as he turned toward grey smoke at tree's edge. Gabe was hurriedly reloading. He spun the trigger guard to drop the breech open, stuffed a patched ball in the breech, poured the powder, and spun the trigger guard to close. He eared back the hammer and was bringing the rifle to his shoulder when he saw the big muzzle of the bull snorting through the brush on a rampaging charge directly toward him. He lifted the rifle and quickly blasted the beast just under his chin, the lead missile blossoming red on the broad chest, but the bull was barely slowed in his charge.

Gabe dove under the long branch of the ponderosa and into the thicket of kinnikinnick, keeping a tight grip on the rifle. He grabbed at his belt pistol as he rolled to his back. The big bull had passed the ponderosa and turned, head down, snorting and pawing the dirt before him. He spotted Gabe in the brush and started his charge. As he neared, Gabe rolled to the side and fired the first barrel as the beast stormed through the brush. He scored a hit, drawing blood on the neck just behind the flopping ear. The bull staggered, but snorted again and he turned, more slowly this time, but his eyes showed fire as he lowered the massive antlers for another charge. Gabe had spun the barrels on the pistol and brought it to full cock, then spun the trigger guard on the Ferguson to open the breech. He worked at loading the rifle by feel, keeping his eyes on the bull. He spun the trigger guard to close the breech but dropped the rifle as the bull charged. Gabe had already picked out his landing place before the bull moved, and with no more than four strides the head and antlers split the brush as he crashed through. Gabe fired just as the bull's head showed, and the bullet shattered the beast's skull, painting the forehead with a half-inch round hole. Gabe dove to the side, and the monster bull fell forward, smashing the brush and pinning Gabe's foot beneath him

Gabe grabbed at his rifle, closed the breech, put powder in the pan and brought it to full cock. But the bull lay still and quiet. Gabe breathed deep, and once he caught his breath, he lay the rifle aside and pushed and pulled to free his moccasined foot. Just as he freed himself, he heard Ezra, "Like you said, he took a lotta killin'!"

Gabe chuckled, looking around at the scene. The ground was torn up, the brush flattened, the lower branches of the ponderosa were broken, all giving the impression there had been a herd of buffalo come through. He slowly stood, shook his head, and said, "I'm gonna enjoy those steaks!"

They turned as they heard the approach of the horses and

stood smiling as the women rode up to the small clearing. Otter jumped down and ran to Gabe, looking around as she neared, then quickly signed, "I was afraid for you!"

He grinned, chuckled, and drew her close beside him as they both looked at the big bull. The cow and yearling had disappeared into the trees and were long gone, but the bull would provide many things for the coming winter. Otter signed, "There will be much meat for us," and motioned to Grey Dove to join her as they both drew knives from scabbards at their waist and started for the carcass. Gabe glanced at Ezra, and both men nodded, having noticed Otter's use of the words, '. . . for us.' Then turned to the carcass to help with the big job of dressing out the bull and getting it back to the cabin. A lot of meat required a lot of work, but they were up to it, considering they had a lot of help.

33 / Colors

As Gabe stepped through the door of the cabin, an unfamiliar nip in the air caused him to slap his arms and hands together and a shiver slid up his spine. "Brrr!" He lifted his eyes to the mountains that pillared the grey light of early morning, their granite peaks catching the first rays of sunshine that crowned their hoary heads. He walked away from the cabin and into the cluster of junipers, hurrying his morning stay to return to the warmth of the night fire. As he stepped into the cabin, he stomped his feet, shivering from the unexpected cold. The thin air of the mountains held the layer of cold close to the ground, signaling the onset of fall. He walked to the fireplace and stoked the fire then stood rubbing his hands together to warm up a tad.

Ezra groaned and stretched then came from his blankets to stand beside his friend. "What's got you goin' on so?" he asked.

"It's cold out there!" declared Gabe, finally relaxing in the warmth as he reached for the coffee pot. He lifted it, shook it, and set it down on the hearth to push it close to the fire. He scooped up a pair of cups, filled them with fresh water, and dumped it into the pot with a small handful of fresh grounds. Coffee was too precious to throw out and start over, it was best just to add to and savor the mature flavor, even if it was blacker than midnight and strong enough to curl your hair. He looked at Ezra, "Fall's comin'. I noticed some color among the aspen up the valley. Accordin' to Otter, once the color shows, we can expect snow anytime."

"Ummhmm, but Dove said they sometimes have a false summer that comes after the first frost. Says it can last a month or two and feel just like summertime."

"You don't say. I just figgered once the snow flies, we probably wouldn't see anything green till spring," replied Gabe, touching the coffee pot to see if it was ready.

"We could use some more meat 'fore the real snow comes," suggested Ezra.

Gabe chuckled, "You just wanna go huntin' with Dove again, but I s'pose you're right, we could hang another elk or two in our cooler. Might hafta build another rack, but that's easy enough done. Having that cavern to store the meat makes things mighty handy and with it so big an' all, it helps the villagers too."

Ezra sat staring into the flames, eyes glazed over, and Gabe asked, "Thinkin' about it again are you?"

"Mmmhmm," he answered, unmoving and continuing to stare at the flames.

"You really want to do that, don't you?" asked Gabe.

"I think so, I just can't quit thinkin' about it."

For the past few weeks, the men had spent most of every day with the women. They continued to school one another on the languages of their people, and the more they were able to talk openly with one another, the more they learned about each other. And the more time spent together, the closer they became. It surprised Gabe and Ezra to learn that Pale Otter and Grey Dove were sisters, Otter the older of the two by one winter, but it also explained why the two women were so much alike and got along so well. The four were seldom apart, yet if they were, the couples were together.

"Haven't you been thinkin' about it?" asked Ezra.

"Yeah, can't help but!" answered Gabe. "Are you sure you are ready to make that kind of commitment? I mean, getting' married or joined as they call it, is a big step."

"Look, I know when we were thinkin' about comin' to the mountains, dreaming about exploring the wilderness and all that, we never once thought about havin' women with us, but . . ." he let the thought hang in the air between them for a moment, "whenever I think about ridin' away and leavin' her behind, I just don't like the idea. I think it'd be harder to leave her than anything I've ever done before, and for the life of me, I can't think of any reason not to join up with her!"

"I know what you mean. It's not like we'd be marryin' some society dame that would want to stay at home and primp all the time. These women would come with us and be happy about it, no matter where we went!" extolled Gabe.

"And we've already seen how helpful they can be, after all, they know more about life in the mountains than we do! And they're pretty good hunters themselves!" remarked Ezra.

"So, who we tryin' to convince?" asked Gabe, looking at his friend that sat still staring into the flames, the light reflecting on his wide eyes.

Ezra slowly smiled, turned to Gabe and said, "I dunno. I think I'm convinced. How 'bout you?"

"We'll have to talk to their folks about this, you know that."

"I've been thinkin' 'bout that too. We've got those extra rifles we took off them Frenchies, and plenty of other trade goods. Mebbe if we throw in an elk or two, and maybe some geegaws, they'd be happy."

"So, when do we talk to the women about this?" asked Gabe, wondering why he was yielding to Ezra on all these issues.

"Oh, mebbe we can spend some time while we're huntin' today and kinda feel 'em out on the idea," he suggested, grinning.

"Oh, I think you and I both know how they feel about things. They'd move in today if we'd let 'em," answered Gabe, knowing the way of the Natives differed considerably from the traditions of the so-called civilized society of the cities.

A scratch at the door told of the arrival of the women and the men greeted them with a hug and lingering embrace. The women looked askance at the men who seemed to be somewhat different in their manner this morning but went to the fireplace to start the morning meal, with only a brief glance back at the grinning men.

By first light, they were on the trail on the south facing slope of the Popo Agie valley. The ridges were black, but the gullies and valleys held strips and clusters of aspen that were beginning to show their color. In the fall, the aspen turned a brilliant gold, with some showing tints of orange and even red, but the splashes of color paint a picture unparalleled anywhere. Although the men were used to the eastern hardwoods and their variegated colors, the aspen, when framed by the snowcapped mountains, brilliant blue of the sky and the rugged terrain of the foothills made a panoramic masterpiece on the canvas of the wilderness.

The women chattered about everything and nothing, enjoying their newly gained fluency in the language of the men. Gabe and Ezra responded in the tongue of the Shoshoni; however, they struggled a bit more than the women. But their conversations had revealed many things about one another, and with every revelation they grew closer to one another.

They rode the trail as it dipped in and out of the gullies that carried spring run-off and sprouted with aspen. One wide draw was thick with aspen and the white trunked quakies shook their leaves at the passersby who wended their way through the grove. After cresting a low ridge and crossing over the saddle, they came to a dry lake bed that offered ample graze and water for the horses and they were all ready for a breather after the arduous climb. With a small fire to warm the leftover biscuits and strip steak from breakfast, they were seated on a long-downed ponderosa that stretched from under the forest canopy. It was a cluster of ponderosa that stretched high overhead that offered the shade from the late morning sun, and the four sat quiet for a few moments until a shrill whistle of an elk bugle split the air. Then within moments, another closer by, answered with his own bugle followed by several grunts and the crashing of brush and branches by his antlers. Every sound and movement was meant to intimidate the challenger and the racket made by the one nearby added to the answer.

"That one's close!" declared Gabe, whispering and looking through the timber, searching for the bull.

Another bugle sounded from the far end of the dry lake, and a big bull, antlers arching over his back with the end tines almost touching his rump, danced into the clearing and lifted his head high to sound his challenge again. The grunts that followed, were accompanied by the crashing of his antlers against a standing spar and sounded like the beating of a jungle drum. Then they heard the thunder of hooves as the big bull trotted through the trees, heading for the confrontation on the flat at the head of the lake bed.

They had been impressed by the size of the first bull, but when the one that came from behind them broke from the trees, they were amazed. The majestic beast stood, head high, massive antlers with seven tines on each rack towered over the bull whose cape that draped over his withers and down his shoulders and chest appeared almost black. The tawny coat across his loins and rump glistened in the light as the robe of royalty. His dark legs and head accented his massive size and he stood proudly, almost sneering at his challenger.

He pawed at the ground, shook his head, and glared at the younger but smaller bull. The challenger was not intimidated, but stood proudly before the reigning bull, and tossed his head with its crown of antlers, pawed the ground and lowered his head as he leaned into his charge. He dug his heels into the dirt and lunged forward, the tips of the tines glistening white as he charged. The big bull, made one step back as he lowered his rack, then lunged forward to meet the challenger. The massive racks clashed together with a clatter that echoed across the valley as the roll of thunder. Bellows sounded from the beasts and they pushed and shoved, digging their hooves deep and thrusting with every ounce of strength their chests and legs could muster. The younger bull leaned into his thrust but was countered with the greater weight of the big bull, then he gave as the beast dug deeper and forced him to give ground.

The massive antlers clattered and crashed, the bulls bellowing, grunting, digging with all their strength, and every sound echoing across the valley. A bald eagle circled overhead, screaming his encouragement to the combatants, while squirrels chattered in the treetops, scolding the beasts for disturbing their day. Suddenly the racks were loosed and both bulls stepped back, sides heaving, tongues lolling. The big bull lifted his head high, shook his antlers side to side, and bellowed at his challenger. He took a step back, another, then his muscles rippled as he gathered his strength, slowly leaning into his charge and with eyes flaring, slobbers flying and head down he charged. The resulting crash echoed again, and the bellowing bulls dug deep, pushing and shoving, one giving, then the other, both determined to conquer his foe, but neither yielding. Again, they separated, heads hanging and sides heaving.

The big bull lifted his head high and glared at the challenger. He cocked his head just a little, and suddenly dropped his rack and lunged. This time the antlers did not lock, the big bull having twisted his head just enough for his brow tines to straddle the smaller bull's and dig a deep gouge in the forehead of the challenger. Blood showed and streamed down between the bull's eyes, but the big bull continued his push and drove the smaller one to the ground. With another shove, a rattle of the antlers, another jab at the side of the downed bull, the big beast vanquished the challenger. He stepped back, tossed his head and grunted and let the challenger rise. The defeated bull staggered a step, turned away and disappeared into the trees. The big bull of the woods lifted his head and bugled the announcement that he was the reigning monarch of the glen and he would soon gather his herd. With another toss of his head, he crashed through the brush as he trotted away.

"Wow! That was somethin'!" declared Gabe. He looked at Otter, "Have you seen a battle like that before?"

"No, but I've known of them. This is the time when the bulls gather the cows for the naa-mea', or moon of the rut. They will breed all the cows in their herd, and next spring, there will be many new calves. It is the way of the wilderness," she explained.

Gabe looked at Ezra, let a slight grin tug at the corners of his mouth, then looked at Otter. “Uh, we’ve been meaning to talk to you two about this winter that’s coming. We think we ought to talk to your father about . . . well, about getting his permission to have a marrying ceremony.” Gabe had been looking directly at Otter as he spoke, and he watched the change in her expression from a slight frown to a broad smile that brightened her eyes and split her face. She clasped her hands and shrugged her shoulders, speechless for the first time since they met. He grinned, and asked, “Would that be all right with you?”

She nodded her head enthusiastically, twisting on her seat and looking to Grey Dove who looked at Ezra. Ezra said, “How ‘bout you, Dove? Would that be alright?”

“Do you mean is it alright for Gabe and Otter?” she asked, slightly confused and concerned.

“No, no. Would it be alright with you if I talked to your father about us, you and me,” he motioned with his hand toward himself and her.

She smiled just as brightly as her sister and nodded just as enthusiastically. The women hugged each other as Gabe and Ezra looked at one another and shrugged. Then the women turned to their men and threw their arms around their necks and gave a long and lingering kiss that neither wanted to stop, but they soon pulled back and looked at each other, smiling and laughing, rejoicing together at what their future would hold.

34 / Trade

The assortment of goods spread on the blanket held Red Pipe and his woman transfixed and staring. Black Bear, who was so named not because of any vision or feat of bravery but because she resembled her name sake, chattered to her man as she pointed at the goods. Two Kentucky styled flintlock rifles lay at the top, with powder horns and possibles pouches beneath. Two butcher knives, two metal combs, and a pile of buttons stretched across the blanket in a row.

Strings of blue and white beads formed another pile next to a pair of tomahawks and bricks of verdigris and vermilion. Beneath it all were two folded blankets that held spools of thread and two mirrors. By any standard this was a pile of riches and would be suitable for a day of trading with the entire village, but this was the offering to the father and mother of Pale Otter and Grey Dove for the women to be given in marriage.

Although Black Bear was animated in her excitement,

Red Pipe sat stoically, glancing occasionally to the trove before him. He looked at Gabe, "You want to take my daughter, Pale Otter for your woman?"

"Yes," he answered, forcing himself to sit quiet and reserved.

"I have heard of other white men, the French traders, who take a woman for one winter and leave. Is that what you want? Someone to warm your blankets for the coming winter?"

"No. I want her to be my woman for all time. Like you and Black Bear," answered Gabe, nodding to the woman who was anxious to touch and hold the beads and more. He chuckled as he saw her elbow her man to hurry up with the trade.

Red Pipe scowled at his woman, looked back at Gabe, "Women can be hard to deal with, never happy and often angry. Are you sure you want that?"

Gabe couldn't help but grin and dropped his eyes to his crossed legs then looked back at Red Pipe, "Every woman is different, but I believe Pale Otter will be a good wife."

Red Pipe grunted, looked at Ezra, "And you want Grey Dove?"

"Yes."

"You are like the buffalo. The bulls of the buffalo take many cows as their own. Is that what you want?"

Ezra shook his head, "No, she will be my only woman."

"Why? Sometimes it is good to have more than one woman. They warm your blankets and cook. When you take many buffalo, they help each other to scrape hides and more."

"She will have her sister near," answered Ezra, fidgeting a little.

"Our daughters have helped their mother with her duties, but now you will take both away. What are we to do? My woman will need help."

Ezra grinned, "Then maybe you should take another woman to your lodge."

Black Bear glowered at Ezra and for a moment he thought she was going to be true to her name and come after him like a mad mama bear, but she elbowed Red Pipe and threatened him with her most dour expression.

Gabe said, "With this," sweeping his hand over the trade goods, "you can pay someone to help your woman. You will be rich in goods and your woman will be the most treasured of all."

Black Bear smiled, nodded and leaned over to say something to Red Pipe. He nodded and looked back at Gabe and Ezra, paused a moment, then said, "It is good," and rose to return to his lodge. Black Bear immediately started gathering up the goods and taking them into the tipi, with only a quick glance over her shoulder at the two men.

Gabe looked at Ezra and both men stood and left the village. Pale Otter and Grey Dove were waiting at the cabin when they returned and the anxious women, although they tried to be reserved and calm, were too excited to wait and battered the men with questions about their father and mother and what their response was to the trade.

"Well, your father thought we should get more than one

woman each," declared Ezra, trying his best to appear indifferent.

"Yeah, and your father offered to let us have both of you kinda on a trial run just for the winter!" added Gabe.

The girls stood back, crestfallen and staring at the men, until the men could no longer keep up the pretense and started laughing. Both women pounded playfully on their man's chest until they held them close and kissed long and hard. The women pulled back, looked at each other smiling, and turned to the men and Otter said, "We must go. We have much to do to prepare for the ceremony." And out the door they went, running and laughing down the slope toward the village.

Gabe looked at Ezra and said, "Looks like we done it this time!"

Ezra chuckled, "Yep, it do! I wonder if anybody'll tell us the details about this ceremony, you know, like when and where."

"Oh, I'm sure we'll be getting a caller that will give us the details. But from what the women said, it's not as involved as it is back in the city."

"That's a relief," replied Ezra.

A scratch at the door told of a visitor and Ezra opened the door to Singing Bird. The girl had a broad smile as she entered and jumped up to give Ezra a hug and ran to Gabe to give him a similar greeting. When the three sat at the table, Bird said, "Otter told me that you," nodding to Gabe, "and you," nodding to Ezra, "will be taking her and her sister as your women. I am happy for you!" she declared. "Otter has asked that I tell you what will happen now."

The men looked at one another, nodded slightly and sat back to listen. Bird twisted on her chair as she began, "First, the women will spend time preparing their dresses and receiving instruction from the older women of the village. This will take two or three days. Then, the Shaman will come for you and you will go into a sweat lodge to purify yourselves. Then you will be given new tunics that you will wear for the ceremony. The Shaman will bring you together and you will be given vows and you must abide by them."

"So, when will all this happen?" asked Ezra.

"Maybe three suns."

Gabe reached for Bird's hand, looked at her and said, "What about you, Bird. Will you be alright?"

She smiled at her friend, nodded her head and answered, "Yes. Nanawu has taken us as her own, and she is a good woman." She looked up at Gabe, smiling, "And in the time of greening, we will go to the Grand Encampment where all the bands will be together. We are told of a new dance, called the Sun Dance, and it will be a good time to be together. Nanawu said that is also a time when young people of all the bands come together and often find their life mates. Although I am too young now, she said she will help me in my search for a life mate, and perhaps he will be at the encampment," she smiled at her friends, excitement showing in her eyes.

"That will be good for you Bird. We are happy for you,"

answered Gabe. He looked at Ezra and added, "And it sounds like we've got some work to do also."

Ezra frowned, "What?"

Gabe nodded to their bunks and said, "I figger we oughta put a partition between there," pointing to the back of the cabin, "and maybe make that into two rooms. I'm thinkin' the women might like a little privacy."

Ezra grinned, "You're probably right. So, I guess we need to get to work."

35 / Ceremony

The Shaman, Big Crow, sat silently at the end of the crowded sweat lodge. It was little more than a hide covered small canopy, barely big enough for the three men sitting almost shoulder to shoulder. Steam rose in a dense cloud, filling the small room, the hot rocks hissed, and the sweat rolled down their backs, chests, and faces. Gabe and Ezra did not know what was expected, but the Shaman sat stoically, watching the men, waiting. The heavy air filled their lungs, but the moist heat made breathing difficult and Gabe arched his back, trying to give room for his lungs to expand. Although it had been just a few moments, they thought it had been most of an hour, the only light coming from the glow of the coals beneath the rocks and a thin slit at the edge of the overhanging hide at the entry.

The lodge sat on the banks of the Popo Agie; the chuckle of the stream barely heard inside the hot canopy, a distant reminder of the coming events. After a short while, Big

Crow scowled at the men, then crawled past them to exit the lodge, motioning for them to follow. Once outside, they stood breathing deeply of the cool air, feeling the nip of the fall air, then at Crow's insistence, followed him to the edge of the river. He did not stop but walked straight into the deep pool in the bend, barking orders to the men to follow, then dropped beneath the water to completely immerse himself in the icy stream. Gabe looked at Ezra, shrugged, and followed the Shaman, shivering with every step and sat down in the cold water, saw the ice forming at the edges, and dropped his head under. Ezra was beside him all the way and did the same. When they both came up, they saw Big Crow climbing the bank where two women waited with blankets. Gabe and Ezra followed, accepted the blankets, wrapped them around their shoulders and stood shivering. The two women, both showing grey in their hair, handed them bundles that held their new tunics for the ceremony.

Big Crow spoke, "Go to your lodge, prepare yourselves and put on the tunics. When you come back, the ceremony will be ready." With a brief dismissal gesture, he turned away and walked toward his lodge near the center of the village.

The entire village had gathered for the ceremony. The Shaman stood before his lodge, arrayed in his ceremonial garb with his hair hanging loosely over one shoulder. A beaded vest held two rows of dyed quills and hung draped over a hair-pipe breastplate. A large necklace with a sizeable turquoise stone embedded in silver hung at his throat. Polished silver bands covered the upper portion of his biceps and his wrists. He held a fan of feathers in his left hand and a gourd rattle in his right. He looked at Gabe and Ezra standing on his left, nodded briefly and started shaking the gourd. Behind them a single drum began beating and Big Crow started a low chant. He looked to the far end of the two groups of people, and the sisters started forward.

The white soft buckskin dresses were similar, but unique. As the women walked gracefully and slowly, side by side, Gabe and Ezra drank in the image of beauty. Otter had knee high moccasins with intricate beading of blue, white, and a little red, that covered the toes and danced up the sides, accenting the thin fringe. Silver conchos held them tight at the ankle and at the top cuff. Her dress had wide rows of blue beads and multi-colored quills at the yoke that gave a picture of the mountains and the sky and clouds above. The row of trade bells accented the ivory elk's teeth that bounced with every step. The fringe at the sleeves, sides and hem of the dress swished with every breath of wind that foretold the coming cold. Her headband matched and held back the glistening ravens wing hair. Her eyes danced and her smile dimpled her cheeks as she drew nearer.

Grey Dove, more demure in her manner, was none the less beautiful in her dress and matching moccasins. The fringe at her sleeves, hem, and seams, were accented by orange colored tufts of rabbit fur that danced and swayed in the breeze. Orange, yellow and white beads and quills formed a geometric pattern at the yoke and hem of the dress and on the toes and sides of her tall moccasins. Her headband held a single eagle feather, cocked at a jaunty angle that spoke of her seldom seen sense of humor. Her head was slightly down, but her eyes held those of Ezra and sparkled in the bright light of the early afternoon.

The men's tunics held little decoration other than a thin row of beads across the chest. Fringe dangled at the arms and back yoke, and the raw edge at the bottom provided its own decoration. But the men were unconcerned with their own attire for their attention was solely on the women as they drew near. Big Crow motioned Otter to his right, then Gabe, and Dove and Ezra to his left.

The Shaman motioned for the couples to link arms and look at him. He looked at the women and began, "You have been given to these men to become their women. You are to do as they say. You are to cook for them, make a home for them, and do all that must be done to meet the need of your man. If you do not do this and obey him, you will bring dishonor upon your family and your people. Do you understand what has been said?"

The women both nodded and answered in the tongue of the Shoshoni, "Yes."

"And do you make an oath to do these things?"

Again they answered with a simple, "Yes."

Big Crow turned toward the men, "You have given much to the family of these women. That has shown the value you have for these women. You will provide for them and protect them in all ways. You will have this woman and only this woman as your own. You will never bring dishonor upon her or her family by anything you do, or anything you fail to do." He paused a moment and said, "You choose to live in the mountain like the bear. Will your women live there with you?"

"Yes, they will," answered Gabe and was echoed by Ezra.

"Do you agree with what I have told you that you are to do as the men of your lodge?"

"Yes," answered Gabe and Ezra together, nodding.

Big Crow handed the rattle to Otter and the fan to Dove. He slipped a knife from a sheath at his waist and reached for Otter's hair and cut a long lock, wrapped it around his finger then stepped to Gabe and did the same. He stood before them and tied the two locks together then placed them in the right pocket of his vest. The Shaman repeated his action with Dove and Ezra, placing their lock in his left pocket. He stood before them again, took the rattle and the fan, and spoke, "These bands of your hair will be hidden. They are the symbol of your joining. If you ever want to no longer be joined, you must first find these locks, and untie them before you can undo your joining."

Crow nodded to the drummer that stood beside his lodge and at his beginning beat, Crow said, "You are now joined," and started to chant with a slight shuffling step. The rest of the village joined in and Otter and Dove nudged their men to start to the cabin. As they walked together, the entire village continued with the dance and walked alongside the new couples, chanting and dancing all the way to the door of the cabin. Once they opened the door and started to enter, the people stopped, shouted encouragement and good wishes, yet were surprised when Gabe and Ezra picked up the women and carried them into the cabin. Once inside, Otter slowly closed the door, and turned back to her man. Ezra and Dove were already embracing, and Gabe took Otter in his arms and kissed her. When they pulled back, he said, "Welcome home, Mrs. Stonecroft!"

Otter smiled, then frowned at the name, but with Gabe smiling and Ezra laughing, the four hugged one another and laughed as they began the new chapter of their lives together. Ezra looked at Gabe, "So, I reckon it's not going to be such a cold winter, after all!"

A LOOK AT: RAIDERS OF THE ROCKIES (STONECROFT SAGA 5)

AUTHOR OF THE BEST-SELLING ROCKY MOUNTAIN SAINT SERIES, B.N. RUNDELL, TAKES US ON AN EPIC JOURNEY IN BOOK FIVE OF THE STONECROFT SAGA.

By any measure, they would be considered old-timers in the mountains of the uncharted territory. Land that had been known as French Louisiana and Spanish Colonial Louisiana, was largely unexplored. The two old-timers were young men that had spent the last two years in that uncharted territory and had taken women from the Shoshone people as their brides. But their long-held dream and goal was to discover and explore the vast lands of the western wilderness and they set out to do just that. But when renegade Coureur des bois of the Hudson's Bay Company and trappers of the Northwest company decide to abandon the fur companies and seek their fortune by raiding the native villages, the two young friends and their women stand in their way.

But the raiders and their renegade Indian scouts will not be dissuaded and set out to pillage and rampage their way through the lands of the Assiniboine, Crow, and Shoshone, letting nothing or no one stand in their way. Even the two men, experienced in the wilderness though they were, would they be a match for a much larger band of raiders and renegades? The life and death struggle will bathe the wilderness in the blood of both raiders and explorers, and the screams of the tortured will echo through the canyons of the wilds.

ABOUT THE AUTHOR

Born and raised in Colorado into a family of ranchers and cowboys, B.N. Rundell is the youngest of seven sons. Juggling bull riding, skiing, and high school, graduation was a launching pad for a hitch in the Army Paratroopers. After the army, he finished his college education in Springfield, MO, and together with his wife and growing family, entered the ministry as a Baptist preacher.

Together, B.N. and Dawn raised four girls that are now married and have made them proud grandparents. With many years as a successful pastor and educator, he retired from the ministry and followed in the footsteps of his entrepreneurial father and started a successful insurance agency, which is now in the hands of his trusted nephew. He has also been a successful audiobook narrator and has recorded many books for several award-winning authors. Now finally realizing his life-long dream, B.N. has turned his efforts to writing a variety of books, from children's picture books and young adult adventure books, to the historical fiction and western genres

https://wolfpackpublishing.com/b-n-rundell/

Lightning Source UK Ltd.
Milton Keynes UK
UKHW012024120122
397037UK00004B/1196

9 781647 344979